SECRETS OF A SHY SOCIALITE

BY
WENDY S. MARCUS

MILLS &
BOON

First published in Great Britain 2013
by Mills & Boon, an imprint of Harlequin (UK) Limited.
Harlequin (UK) Limited, Eton House, 18-24 Paradise Road,
Richmond, Surrey TW9 1SR

© Wendy S. Marcus 2013

ISBN: 978 0 263 89872 9

Harlequin (UK) policy is to use papers that are natural, renewable and recyclable products and made from wood grown in sustainable forests. The logging and manufacturing process conform to the legal environmental regulations of the country of origin.

Printed and bound in Spain
by Blackprint CPI, Barcelona

CRAVING HER SOLDIER'S TOUCH is dedicated to Army Specialist Adam Bivins and to men and women around the world who risk their lives to fight for the freedom of others. SECRETS OF A SHY SOCIALITE is dedicated to Mary Ritter and Stella Turk: two vibrant, courageous and strong women whom I am honored to call my friends.

With special thanks to:

My wonderful editor, Flo Nicoll, for believing in me and always helping me find my way when I veer off track.

My supportive husband, for calling from work at the end of each day to ask what he should pick up for dinner.

My three loving children, for making me proud of the wonderful people they are growing up to be. I am truly blessed.

CHAPTER ONE

IF THERE was an easy way to explain why she'd impersonated her identical twin sister, lured a man into bed under semi-false pretenses, then left town without a word to anyone, and not come off sounding like an insincere, inconsiderate, immoral hussy, it required more brain power and finesse than Jena Piermont had at her disposal.

"You've been home for two weeks," Jaci, Jena's twin, said, leaning back on the sofa and lifting her fuzzy-slippered feet onto the coffee table. "I think I've been pretty patient, but it's time for answers."

Past time. Where had she been? Why did she leave? How long would she be staying? And the biggie: whose genetic contribution was partly responsible for her adorable six-week-old twin baby girls? Jaci didn't know enough to ask about the impersonation part of Jena's explanation dilemma. Soon enough.

"I'm almost done." Jena arranged the baked brie and slices of crusty French baguette on two large plates and added them to the tray holding the crudité and *pâté de foie gras*. Never let it be said that Jena Piermont, of the Scarsdale, New York, Piermonts, was not a consummate hostess. Even while hosting her own fall from grace.

Now, to reveal the truth before the other invitees arrived at their little pow-wow. Unfortunately the news she most wanted to share, to discuss with her sister and get her advice on—the real reason she'd returned to town and would be staying for a few weeks—had to remain secret. If everything went as planned, fingers crossed, she could pull it off without Jaci ever finding out.

Jena swallowed then used a napkin to blot the unladylike clamminess from her palms. Grace under pressure. She inhaled a fortifying breath, lifted the tray and carried it to the coffee table. "Move your feet." She arranged the delectable treats beside the sparkling water and bottled beer.

Justin liked his beer.

"Stop," Jaci said. "You always do this when you get nervous. Flit around, straightening up, preparing snacks."

Jena dropped the pillow she'd been in the process of plumping and rearranging on the loveseat.

"Just sit down." Jaci patted the sofa beside her. "Tell me why you've been so quiet lately. What has you so upset? Before the guys get here."

The guys. Jena considered excusing herself and running to the bathroom to vomit. But that would waste precious time. So she sat. She could do this, would do this. "I love you," she reminded Jaci.

"I love you, too," Jaci said, studying her. "Why do you look like you've got an olive stuck in your throat?"

Because that's how she felt. Okay. No sense putting it off any longer. Tonight was the night. "Justin is the father," Jena blurted out, her gaze fixed on her lap. "Of the twins," she clarified—as if clarification was needed.

Usually talkative Jaci sat mute.

Jena peered over at her. "Say something," she prompted.

"I'm…surprised. That's all." Jaci shifted on the couch to face her. "I knew you had a crush on him in high school."

Not really a crush. More like a fascination-attraction-day/night dreamy type thing for the totally wrong type of boy. A silent plea for rescue from a mundane existence cluttered with more responsibilities than any teenager should be burdened with. An illicit mental visit to the dark side where the expectations and judgment of others meant nothing and Jena could indulge in the forbidden. Break the rules. Go wild. Have imaginary sex.

"And I'd thought maybe you were considering him as a husband candidate to meet the terms of our trust," Jaci went on.

Never. Okay. Maybe once, or a few times during random episodes of pregnancy-induced psychosis when out-of-control hormones caused gross mutations to the brain cells responsible for rational thought. Moments of weakness when Jena had actually entertained the possibility of Justin protecting her from the machinations of her brother, providing a home for her and their daughters, and taking care of the three of them.

But Justin didn't want her, and Jena refused to be any man's second best, which didn't much matter right now, anyway, since getting married no longer occupied the top spot on her list of priorities. Staying alive for her daughters did.

"I had no idea you two were…" Jaci began. "I mean, I haven't seen you together in years. Neither of you mentioned that you…kept in touch."

They didn't, not technically, unless stalking him on

social networking sites counted. Some childhood habits—like an unhealthy interest in all things Justin—
were hard to break. Jena picked at a chipped fingernail
she kept forgetting to file down, preoccupied with caring for the twins and worrying about the future and Jaci
being attacked… "It was one night." She couldn't look
at her sister. "We met up at Oliver's." A favorite restau-
rant/bar where Justin and Jaci often hung out. And now
for the worst of it. "He thought I was you."

"What?" Jaci screeched. "You did *not* just say Justin
took you to bed thinking you were me."

She couldn't change what'd happened or the outcome. All she could do was own up to it. She looked
Jaci in the eye. "It was the anniversary of Mom's death.
I'd had a horrible fight with Jerald." Their pompous,
older half-brother who'd been aggressively trying to
manipulate them into marrying any one of a dozen of
his equally pompous business associates. "I had to get
out of the house." A.k.a. the Piermont Estate where she
and Jerald each had a wing. "We'd spoken earlier and
you were still so depressed over Ian returning to Iraq.
I decided to surprise you with dinner." And that's how
it'd started, with a kind gesture to cheer her sister.

"I ordered a glass of wine while I waited for the
takeout and noticed Justin sitting across the bar. Alone.
With a couple of empty, upside down shot glasses lined
up in front of him." Normally she would have simply
blended into the crowd and stared at him from afar, attraction battling better judgment. But, "One of the bar-
tenders noticed me and called out, 'Jaci, take him home
before I toss him out of here.'" Boy had Justin perked
up at the mention of Jaci's name. "At the time, it didn't

seem to matter who he thought I was, as long as I got him home safely."

"You mean to tell me," Jaci crossed her arms over her chest and stared at Jena, "during the ride in the Piermont limo, the walk from the parking lot up to the fifth floor, and while you were stripping off each other's clothes it never crossed your mind that maybe you should clue him in to your real identity?"

Of course it had. But close proximity to Justin had caused an arousal spike that forced it away and relegated it to the spot where she stored all the unwelcome thoughts and memories she'd accumulated through the years, corralled deep in the recesses of her brain. Instead she'd allowed herself to enjoy his company and the freedom that came with pretending to be Jaci who balked at the rules and did and said what she wanted, when she wanted. Just like Justin.

For the first time in her life, Jena didn't overanalyze, didn't weigh the pros and cons or think about what a person of good moral character would do. Instead she'd focused on what she'd wanted, what she'd needed more than anything at that specific moment in time—comfort, a caring touch, a brief sojourn from real life—without a care for the consequences. And look where it'd gotten her. "I'm sorry."

"It makes no sense." Jaci said, pulling a pillow onto her lap and playing with the fringe. "Justin and I don't have that kind of relationship. We're friends. We've *never*..." She grimaced. "I have to admit I'm a little weirded out by the whole thing."

"If it helps, I made the first move." An orchestrated meeting of their lips. Jena leaned forward to try to catch Jaci's attention. "He tried to stop me." A half-hearted,

'We shouldn't,' milliseconds before he'd yanked her close and kissed her with the unbridled passion of a man releasing years of pent up attraction and lust.

Jaci smiled. "You little tigress. I didn't know you had it in you."

It'd been a quite a shocker to Jena, too.

Someone knocked on the door. Jena jumped.

"Quick," Jaci said. "Why did you take off?"

"The next morning Justin went nuts, carrying on about what a mistake it'd been. Angry at himself for letting it happen, for ruining your friendship. Guilty because you were Ian's girl and he didn't poach." Jena shivered at the memory of Justin in a rage, which was why she'd chosen to tell him about the twins with Jaci close by. "I knew I had to tell him. And I did."

Him sitting on the side of the bed elbows on his thighs, his head in his hands, completely comfortable with his nakedness. Her standing in the doorway to the bedroom, fully dressed. "I said, 'You didn't have sex with Jaci, you had it with me. Jena.' Rather than a whew or a yippee, he'd tilted his miserable face up, oh so slowly, and simply said, 'Oh, God. That's even worse.'"

"Oh, honey. I'm sorry." Jaci reached for her hand and squeezed.

"Wait, it gets better," Jena said. "Then he'd slapped his hand over his mouth and with a muffled, 'I think I'm going to be sick,' he ran past me and threw up in the bathroom." Intimacy with Jena had nauseated him to the point of regurgitation.

Another knock. Louder.

"Be right there," Jaci yelled.

"So I left."

"Why didn't you come to me?"

Jena looked away. "I was humiliated and disgusted with myself. How could I face you? I'm so ashamed."

"Hey," Jaci said. "Look at me." When Jena did she asked, "Where did you go?"

Jena saw understanding in Jaci's eyes and felt hope that they'd get past this. "Home." Where she'd given the guard at the gate strict instructions not to let anyone up the drive. As if Justin would have wasted his time coming after her. Within three hours she'd made the necessary arrangements, packed and was being chauffeured to the airport. "South Carolina. Marta's there." Their old nanny. "When Jerald sent her away she'd said she'd always be there for us." And boy had Jena appreciated Marta's calm reassurance when faced with an unexpected pregnancy complicated by yet another painful lump in her right breast, her caring support while dealing with the fear of diagnostic testing adversely affecting her unborn babies through the results of yet another needle biopsy, and her knowledgeable guidance leading up to the birth of the twins through surviving those first few sleep-deprived weeks.

"I'm so glad," Jaci stood, pulled Jena up to her feet and hugged her. "But why didn't you tell me? All this time I'd been so worried you were alone and struggling."

Jena shrugged. "If you knew, there'd have been no keeping you away. You have so many people depending on you. The residents of the Women's Crisis Center." Which Jaci had founded. "Your patients." Through the community health agency where she worked. "I couldn't take you away from all the good you do simply because of the mess I'd made of my life."

"I love you, Jena. And while I'd prefer it if you have

sex as yourself and not me, I will always love you." She
stepped back and looked into Jena's eyes. "There's nothing you could ever do to change that."

"Thank you." Jena held back tears. Barely.

Another knock and an, "Open the door, Jaci," Ian
demanded. "Are you okay?"

Jaci wiped the corner of her eye with a knuckle.
"He's such a worrywart." But she smiled when she said
it.

"Justin's with him," Jena reminded her. "He doesn't
know I'm back." And since she was staying with Jaci,
who lived in the same luxury high-rise, she'd rarely left
the condo in order to keep it that way. The one time in-
teraction had been unavoidable, at the benefit for the
Women's Crisis Center, she'd pretended to be Jaci and
he hadn't given her a second look.

Jaci raised her eyebrows and sucked in a breath between her teeth. "Oh, boy."

"You got that right." Girding herself to face the
men, well, one of the men, waiting in the hallway, Jena
walked to open the door.

And there he stood. Justin Rangore. *Magnificent.*
Tall. Dark-haired. Broad-shouldered. Muscled in all
the right places. The perfectly maintained goatee he'd
had since the eleventh grade. She fought off a tremble
of delight at the tingly memory of him rubbing it against
her neck and nipples and…lower. God help her.

"He made it sound like you were a mess," Justin said,
sliding a roughened finger from her temple, down her
cheek to her chin. "But you look beautiful as always."

No. Jaci was the beautiful one, the perfect one. Even
though they were identical to the point only a handful
of people could tell them apart—two of them, their par-

ents, dead—whenever Jena looked in the mirror imper-
fections and inadequacies overshadowed pretty.

The same old ache in her chest flared anew. He didn't
recognize her, never recognized her. Once again he'd
failed to look deep enough to see the unique individual,
separate from her popular, outgoing, life-of-the-party
look alike. More than a privileged Piermont, a member
of the social elite in a town fixated on status. More than
the quiet, studious, rule-follower and people-pleaser
others saw her to be. Jena. A woman, who deserved to
be loved and respected and noticed for who she was.
Not as philanthropic or wonderful as Jaci, but kind and
caring and loyal in her own right.

Ian, Jaci's fiancé of twenty-four hours, who had no
problem telling the two of them apart, stood beside
Justin, shaking his head in disappointment. "She looks
beautiful because she's not the one exposed to pep-
per spray in an elevator yesterday, you ignoramus." Ian
walked toward her, placed a hand on her shoulder and
squeezed in support. "Hey there, future sister-in-law,"
he said and slid past her into Jaci's condo.

"Jena?" Justin asked, baffled, searching her face for
some identifier for confirmation.

How she'd longed to hear him utter her name that
night, in the dark, in the heat of passion. Instead he'd
tortured her with each, *"Damn, Jaci, you feel so good."*
Punished her with, *"You are so special, Jaci. Do you
have any idea how special you are?"*

"Hi, Justin," she said. "Come on in." She turned to
the side to make room for him. "Let's get this over
with."

He took one long-legged step forward and stared

down at her. "We need to talk," he said quietly, stating the obvious.

He stood too close, his deep brown eyes serious, his expression solemn, his scent making her weak, making her crave... "That's why you're here." She backed into the condo, needed space, air. "To talk." To have the conversation she should have initiated during her first week back in town. But appointments with doctors, hospitals and attorneys, taking care of the twins, and ensuring their futures had taken precedence.

He leaned in close. "Alone."

So he could berate her for what she'd done? He couldn't make her feel worse than she already did. To ask her to keep the circumstances of what'd happened between them a secret? Too late. "Jaci knows," Jena said.

Justin stared down at Jena's deceptively beautiful face. If only she had the personality to match. Shoulder length blonde curls, her complexion flawless, her eyes a striking blue. So much like Jaci's but different. Softer, yet guarded. Funny, he couldn't remember ever getting close enough to notice the difference before. Jena usually hung in the background. Quiet. Boring. A goodie-goodie, judgmental, rich-bitch snob. Not at all his type.

But something had changed in the ten or so months she'd been gone. She stood taller, more confident. Attractive. Alluring.

The words 'Jaci knows' brought him back to the conversation.

Crap. If Jaci knew that meant Ian knew, or would know soon. Ian would pound him senseless for sure. Justin wouldn't fight back because he deserved it and, under the circumstances, would do the exact same thing if a friend he trusted took a woman he cared about to bed. Strangely, rather than apprehension at what was sure to escalate into a full blown physical altercation with one of his best—and strongest—friends, he felt relief.

But that didn't mean he wouldn't try to deter Ian with an explanation. "It's not what you think." Justin walked into Jaci's condo. Jena closed the door behind him.

Jaci gave him a wary, perplexed look. He'd avoided revealing the truth for that exact reason. She was his best female friend. Hell, his only female friend. And they'd been getting into trouble together and looking out for one another since junior high school. He loved her. Like a sister. "I can explain."

Ian went on guard. "Explain what?" he asked.

"Come on." Jaci took Ian by the hand and tugged him toward the bedroom.

"Wait." Justin stood firm. It was time to come clean. "I slept with Jena."

Uninterested, Ian turned to follow Jaci.

"At the time I'd thought she was Jaci," Justin admitted.

Ian jerked to a stop.

"And there's no way you would have slept with plain, boring, inexperienced Jena otherwise," Jena snapped. "Am I right?" She crossed her arms over her chest and glared at him.

He'd deal with her in a minute. "Jaci was so upset when you ran out on her," he spoke to Ian who turned around to face him. "Moping around. She didn't want to do anything, go anywhere. I hadn't seen her that depressed since right after her dad died and her mom was injured. That was your fault, not mine." He pointed at Ian.

"So you thought you'd cheer her up with some naked fun while I was off fighting a war?" To someone who didn't know Ian, he'd seem eerily calm. But Justin could tell when he was about to blow.

How to explain... "I'd come off a lousy shift. A woman and her seven-year-old daughter, missing for thirty-six hours. Found dead. Brutalized." Tossed in a Dumpster like yesterday's trash. Three years on the police force, patrolling the most dangerous crime ridden area in Westchester County, and that day had made him question his decision to forgo a cushy job in his father's investment company to attend the police academy.

"Oh, Justin." Jena set her palm on the bare skin of his arm. "I had no idea."

Her touch, soft, gentle and feminine, moved him in a way Jaci's never had. But there'd been a few times... "Jaci is my friend," Justin said. "Your girlfriend."

"My fiancée."

"Right." Justin snapped. "Still getting used to that." And wondering how it would affect his friendship with Jaci, if they still had one after tonight. "Anyway. My point is. I don't lust after Jaci. Hell, she's like a sister to me." Their relationship platonic...ninety-nine percent of the time. "But there were a few times back in high school..." When something had shifted, when physical attraction flared between them for a few minutes and they'd given in to its demands. After each encounter Jaci had insisted they never speak of it again, that they pick up the next day as if nothing had happened or risk the ruin of a friendship they both valued.

At the narrowing of Ian's eyes and the clenching of

his fists, Justin thought better of continuing on in that vein. "In my crap state of mind I let alcohol skew my thinking. I needed a distraction. She needed comfort. Or so I'd thought." He glanced at Jena.

"I *did*." Jena looked up at him. "That night would have been my mom's fifty-third birthday." She paused. "What do you mean there were a few times during high school? Times when you were physically attracted to Jaci? Like when?"

"I'd rather not—"

"I'd sure like to know," Jaci said, staring at him.

"Me, too," Ian added, straightening up to his full height.

Of course Justin's cell phone didn't ring. No emergency to run off to. No reason he could think of to turn and leave and never address this topic again.

"Like sophomore year?" Jena asked. "Under the bleachers at the Mt. Vernon Scarsdale men's varsity basketball home game?"

Jaci had dropped her purse. It'd been hot in the gym. Stuffy. Her tee had molded to her full breasts. Her scent had affected him. It'd been the first time being in close proximity to Jaci had elicited a physical response. The first time she'd looked up at him with longing. The first time he'd kissed her.

"I wasn't at that game," Jaci said, looking back and forth between him and Jena.

"It was me," Jena said quietly, not looking at him.

Jaci's holier than thou, prude of a sister? Impossible. "Junior year. The gazebo at the Parks's Fourth of July barbeque," Justin said, remembering a friendly hug after a win at horseshoes that had morphed into a frantic, heated groping session where he'd touched her bare breasts for the first time. And though he'd touched dozens of breasts before them, the smooth, rounded, silkiness of Jaci's, capped off by the hardest, most aroused nipples he'd ever felt, left a lasting impression.

"Me," Jena said, looking at the ground.

That'd been ice-water-in-her-veins Jena hot and breathless and begging for more in response to his touch? No way. "Down by the lake," he went on. "The bonfire after senior skip day." Where they'd paired off out of sight and explored each other's partially clothed bodies to the point of orgasm.

Jena inhaled a deep breath then exhaled and looked up at him apologetically. "Me."

Holy crap.

"Jena Piermont. You little slut," Jaci teased with a smile.

"You used to ask me to pretend to be you an awful lot back then and I got pretty good at it," Jena said to Jaci.

She'd managed to fool him, that's for sure.

"To take a trigonometry test or give an oral presentation," Jena said. "To make an appearance at a party while you went off I don't know where with I don't know who." Jena looked up at him. "I used to fake migraines and lock myself in my room, then climb down the trellis outside my window."

"No wonder I had such a bad reputation," Jaci said. Amused.

"You had a bad reputation because of your big mouth, your wild spirit and your lack of respect for authority. Not because you deserved it," Justin clarified.

"And not because of me," Jena added. "It only happened with Justin."

For some reason that pleased him.

"And it's not going to happen again," Ian asserted himself into the conversation, his eyes focused in on Jena accented with a raised eyebrow. "No more switching places." He moved his gaze to Jaci. "For any reason," he emphasized.

"No," Jena said, shaking her head. Contrite. "Never again. I promise."

Jaci, however, chose not to commit. "Let's go." She took Ian by the hand, again, and tugged him toward the bedroom, again. "They need to talk."

This time Ian allowed himself to be pulled away.

Well that had gone better than expected. Justin felt lighter. Freer. Except now he had to deal with Jena. A girl he'd despised in high school, who, apparently, was the very same girl with whom he'd shared some of the more special boy-girl moments of his teenage years. With Jena, not Jaci.

Jena who used to look down her snobby nose at him.

Jena, who'd enticed him into bed by pretending to be her sister.

"But I made snacks," Jena called after Ian and Jaci, seeming nervous, her confidence slipping.

"I could sure use one of those beers." Lined up on the coffee table. His favorite brand.

Jena rushed to open one and held it out to him.

Ian closed the door to Jaci's bedroom, leaving Justin and Jena alone. He took a swig of brew. Cold. Refreshing.

They stood there in awkward silence.

Justin smiled. "You're no better than all those girls you criticized back in high school, whose reputations you disparaged for dating me."

"Dating you?" she asked, looking him straight in

the eyes. "Don't you mean rubbing up against you and sucking face with you in the hallway of our high school or bragging about giving you oral sex in the boys' locker room and going all the way with you on school grounds?"

Good times.

"I refuse to lump myself in with those girls. But I'm sorry." She fidgeted with a button on her blouse. "I was wrong to let you to believe I was Jaci. It was dishonest and repugnant and I ran away like a coward afterwards." She shook her head. "I am mortified by my behavior."

"And so you should be." Fancy that, Princess Jena Piermont capable of apologizing and offering a convincing show of remorse. "But I think repugnant is taking it a bit far." Because he'd enjoyed every minute of their time together, until the dawn of a new day brought with it insight and hindsight. And a hellacious hangover he would not soon forget.

Now for two issues that had been burning his gut for months. First, "Please tell me you were a virgin." As horrible as it was to think he'd taken her virginity without the care of a knowing, sober bed-partner, the alternative was even worse. That he'd unknowingly been too rough and hurt her. Either way the evidence had stained his sheet.

"I'd rather not—"

"Please," he took her by the arm, gentle but firm, and turned her to face him. He didn't like her, hated the upper class lifestyle she embraced and the elitist, unlikable people she called friends, but she didn't deserve... "The thought that I might have hurt you..." tore him up.

"You didn't," she assured him. "A little pinch from it being my first time, that's all."

"Was it…?" Good. He cursed himself for not remembering every vivid detail.

"It was fine," she said quietly. Shyly.

Justin cringed at her bland choice of adjective. Fine, as in acceptable? Adequate? Nothing special?

"Until the next morning."

When he'd totally lost it. "Yeah, about that. I woke up and noticed the condom from the night before draped over the trashcan beside the bed. With a big slice down the side." And his heart had stopped. "I don't know if it happened before, during or after, but on top of thinking I'd ruined my friendships with Jaci and Ian, I realized there was a chance she, well, you, could get pregnant." He took another swig of beer. "I panicked." How could he have been so carless? So unaware?

"Especially once you'd found out you may have gotten *me* pregnant and not Jaci," Jena said. "If I remember correctly your exact words were, 'Oh, God. That's even worse.'"

Had he really said that out loud? From the hurt look in her eyes, yup, he had. Dammit. "Because we have nothing in common. We don't even like each other. But bottom line," after years of being treated like an afterthought and an inconvenience by his father, his only parent for as long as he could remember, Justin had decided, "I don't want kids. With any woman. Or marriage." He didn't do relationships. Never could manage to give a woman what she needed outside of the bedroom. Too emotionally detached, according to numerous women who'd expected more than he was capable of giving, too self-centered to share his life with another person. Like father like son, apparently. "I like my life the way it is." Women around when he wanted them, gone when he didn't. Doing what he wanted when he wanted, on his own terms, without negotiation, explanation or altercation. "But I handled the possibility that our night together may have had long-term consequences poorly. I'm sorry. You deserved better."

She looked on the verge of tears.

Some unfamiliar instinct urged him to take her into his arms to comfort her.

He resisted.

"Hey. No tears," he said, trying to keep things upbeat. "It all worked out. Wherever you took off to has obviously been good for you. You look great. And no consequences." Now what? He should leave. Except he didn't want to, was still coming to terms with the fact he and Jena had shared some magical moments back in high school. Jena, not Jaci as he'd originally thought, which explained why, after each encounter, she'd so adamantly insisted it never be repeated or spoken of again.

At the sound of a baby crying in the hallway, Jena glanced at her watch and stiffened. "There's…"

The baby's cry grew louder. Someone knocked at the door. "I'd hoped to have a few more minutes to ease into this," Jena said nervously on her way to open the door.

Mandy, the wife of one of Ian's army buddies who'd been killed in Iraq, stood there holding a tiny, red-faced, screaming infant while a second tiny, red-faced, infant squalled from a stroller, and her toddler cried in a kid carrier on her back.

"I'm so sorry," Mandy said. "I know you said seven o'clock, but Abbie's hysterical and we couldn't calm her down. Then she set off Annie. And now Maddie."

Jena reached for the baby in Mandy's arms and a heavy weight of doom settled on Justin's shoulders. No.

"This little consequence's name is Abbie," Jena said brightly holding up the baby dressed in pink. "That one is named Annie." She motioned with her elbow to the stroller where Mandy was unstrapping the baby dressed in yellow. "This is why I asked Ian to bring you down tonight. Now that you know, you can go."

What? Justin opened his mouth to reply, but no words came out. He stood there idly, unable to move, watching Jena, her expression worried as she paced, patting the baby's back, trying to calm her.

Girls. Annie named for Jena's mother. Abbie, for his grandmother? Who'd done her best to impart a mother's love and wisdom, and fill in the gaps left by a disinterested father too busy for his own son. Maybe if she'd lived past his eighth birthday, Justin wouldn't have followed in his father's pleasure seeking footsteps, avoiding attachments and commitments with women.

Twins.

His.

There'd be fathers toasting, high-fiving, and laughing to the point of tears all around the tri-state area when the news got out. *"I can't wait for the day someone like you shows up at your door to take out your daughter. I hope he's as careless with her heart as you've been with..."* Justin couldn't remember the daughter's name. One of dozens of silly girls who'd hung on his every word, offered themselves to him then got their feelings hurt when he didn't reciprocate their professed caring and love.

What goes around comes around.

Justin wanted to run, to close himself in the quiet of his condo, alone to think. But he would not be dismissed like one of her servants. "I'll go when I'm good and ready to go."

"Right," she snapped. "Because you only do what you want when you want with a total disregard for what another person might want."

Maybe so, but she was far from perfect, too. "Unless someone resorts to deceit to get me to do otherwise." He glared at her.

Unaffected by his retort or his scathing look she fired back, "And you're so easy to trick because you're so darn shallow you only see what you want to see, a pretty face and a pair of breasts."

Jaci ran out of the back bedroom, followed by Ian. "What happened?" Jaci asked, taking the baby in yellow from Mandy while Ian lifted Maddie out of her carrier and handed her to her mom.

"Something's got Abbie all worked up and she got the other two crying," Jena explained.

Ian walked over to Justin. "You okay?"

"You knew about the babies and didn't tell me?" Justin asked, finding it hard to breath. No warning? No chance to adjust or digest? To figure out how to respond? What the hell to do?

"Jena wanted to tell you herself."

"How long have you known?" The screaming echoed in his ears. Dread knotted in his gut. Life as he knew it was over.

"Since the benefit for Jaci's crisis center."

Almost two weeks. "Jena was at the benefit?" Justin had run security for the event. How could he have overlooked her?

"You really need to work on telling the two of them apart," Ian said. "It's not all that difficult." After a moment Ian added, "Time to man up and help Jena with your daughters."

Daughters.

Justin didn't want daughters. Didn't want to be a father. Did not want his life to be contorted into something unrecognizable.

CHAPTER TWO

JENA missed Marta something fierce. She bounced Abbie gently while patting her tiny back. Knowing her old nanny had been a few doors down the hall had eased many of Jena's new mother insecurities and fears. Of course the girls had been perfect angels then. Text-book infants.

Nothing like this. Abbie arched her back and let out an unusually shrill cry.

"It's going to be okay, sweetie girl," she whispered against the baby's cheek, hoping hearing the words would make *her* believe them. It didn't work. Jena's heart pounded. *Don't panic. You're a nurse. You can handle this.*

"When did she last eat?" Jena asked Mandy, starting with the most basic reason the twins cried.

"Mrs. Calvin and I fed them about an hour and a half ago."

Moving on to diaper, Jena walked down the hall and set Abbie on the changing table where she writhed and kicked her tiny legs making it difficult to unsnap her outfit.

Diaper dry. Shoot.

Jena stripped off Abbie's clothes and examined her naked body for signs of irritation or anything out of the ordinary. Aside from a red face, the only unusual thing identified during her careful head to toe assessment was a firm, maybe a bit distended, belly.

Please be gas.

"Jaci told me to give you this." Justin walked into the room and handed her a bottle. He stared down at Abbie, still looking a bit shell-shocked.

"I'm sorry you found out like this," Jena said, fastening a new diaper. "I'd planned to give you some warning before—"

A milky-looking fountain spurted from Abbie's mouth. Jena flipped her onto her side and rubbed her back. "Hand me a cloth."

Justin did. "Is she okay?"

"I don't know." Worry seeped into her voice. But maybe after spewing out the contents of her tiny tummy Abbie would feel better.

Wishful thinking, because she sucked in a breath and started to cough and sputter.

"She's choking," Justin so helpfully pointed out, pushing Jena closer to all out panic.

No. *Think like a nurse.* She sat Abbie on the changing table, and, supporting her chin leaned her forward and patted her back.

Airway clear, Abbie's screams turned even more intense, desperate for her mommy to do something to help her. But what?

Helpless tears filled Jena's eyes as she struggled to dress her squirming infant in a soft cotton sleeper. She picked her up and tried to give her the bottle while she hurried back into the living room. Abbie clamped her lips closed and turned her head, refusing the nipple. "How long has she been like this?" Jena asked Mandy.

"A good forty-five minutes before I brought her back. Mrs. Calvin and I tried everything we could think of to calm her."

If Mrs. Calvin, Jaci's upstairs neighbor who'd raised five children and had been helping out with the twins since Jena's return, couldn't solve the problem, Jena had little confidence she'd be able to.

"She said sometimes babies just need to cry," Mandy said.

But not like this. For close to an hour. And what if Jena weren't here to see to the needs of her daughter? Would Abbie's unknown caregiver allow her to cry, alone in her room, for hours and hours, totally unconcerned with her discomfort and distress, thinking 'sometimes babies just need to cry'? Jena's heart twisted uncomfortably. As soon as this was over she'd make a note regarding how she'd like this situation handled in the future, should she not be around to deal with it, knowing there was no guarantee her wishes would be followed. She swallowed a lump of despair.

"We need to get her to a doctor," Justin said in his police voice, taking charge.

"I'll watch Annie," Jaci offered.

"It's probably just gas," Jena said, hoping that was true.

"But you don't know for sure," Justin pointed out.

"No." Jena fought for composure. "I've never quite mastered the ability to read minds," she said, maintaining an even tone. "Even if I had, I imagine reading an infant's mind must be pretty darn difficult considering they haven't yet acquired the skills necessary to communicate."

Justin raised an eyebrow. "So quiet Jena has some bite, and sarcasm is your weapon of choice."

Yup. But she didn't usually speak it out loud. "I don't have a pediatrician in the area yet, which doesn't matter since the office would most likely be closed now, anyway. And Abbie hasn't had all her vaccinations," Jena said. "I can't take her into an emergency room crowded with sick people."

Jena paced and rocked and patted. Abbie screamed. What to do? What to do? A pressure behind her forehead made her eyeballs feel on the verge bulging out of their sockets. An emergency room visit. The absolute worst case scenario. No insurance. Maxed out credit cards. They couldn't turn her away for inability to pay, could they? The humiliation. But this wasn't about her and her stupid choices. This was about Abbie.

"I know a pediatric urgent care center," Justin said. "Twenty minutes away." Perfect. Maybe the car ride would put Abbie to sleep and they wouldn't need to go inside. "I'll need a ride." Jena threw it out there to no one in particular. Pathetic rich girl chauffeured from place to place all her life, she'd never bothered to learn to drive. And at age twenty-four she couldn't even drive her daughter to seek medical treatment.

"I'll take you," Justin said. Before she could tell him she'd rather go with Jaci, or Ian, or Mandy, or anyone but him, he added, "Come on," and headed for the door.

Like a mother of twins could simply run out of the condo on a moment's notice.

Men.

"I have to—"

"Here's a car seat." Ian walked out of the second

bedroom she temporarily shared with the girls. Not all men were as clueless as Justin.

"Diaper bag restocked and ready," Jaci said, holding it out to Justin, who, rather than reaching for it so they could get underway, stared at it like Jaci was trying to pass him a severed limb.

So sorry she hadn't purchased a diaper bag worthy of a macho cop. "I like pink," Jena said, snatching the bag and slinging the strap over her shoulder. "Does the car seat meet with your approval or should I carry that, too?" She shifted Abbie and wrapped her in a baby blanket. Jaci slipped a little pink hat on Abbie's head and gave her a kiss.

"Lord help me," Justin said, taking the car seat from Ian. "I've never seen this side of her. She's got a mouth like Jaci."

Not quite. But Jena smiled, welcomed the comparison, because Jaci stood up for herself. Jaci didn't let people take advantage of her. Jaci could handle anything.

Justin made the twenty minute trip to the pediatric urgent care center in less than fifteen minutes. Apparently speeding, passing on double yellow lines, and ignoring red lights were perks of the police profession. If not for the seatbelt that kept her lower body anchored on the back seat of his SUV, Jena had no doubt she would have been tossed around like a forgotten soccer ball. During the harrowing ordeal she held on to Abbie's car seat which was strapped in beside her, her attempts to sooth her daughter and ignore Justin's aggressiveness behind the wheel both futile.

Abbie's unrelenting crying filled the car, echoed in her head, vibrated through her body.

Justin slowed down—thank you—and turned into the parking lot of a darkened, somewhat rundown strip mall in a not-so-nice part of town. "Why are you pulling in here?" He parked in front of the one lit storefront. The Pediatric Urgent Care Center. "It doesn't look..." Professional. Clean. Safe.

While Jena pondered a way to nicely say, "There is no way I am taking my daughter into that dump," Justin hopped out of the SUV, opened her door, and stuck his head inside. "Now there's the Jena I know. Do you want to take her out of the carrier or bring in the whole thing?"

The Jena he knew? She unstrapped Abbie, removed her from the car seat and cuddled her close as she climbed out. "What's that supposed to mean?" she asked. But she knew. The kids at school mistook quiet, smart and wealthy for snobby, snobby and snobby.

But this had nothing to do with being a snob and everything to do with being a concerned mother who wanted her daughter examined by a qualified practitioner in a well-equipped, high quality medical setting.

Justin set his large hand on her low back and applied a gentle pressure to get her moving toward the glass door. "You don't know me at all," Jena said. Not exactly his fault. No one did. Because in living life to avoid conflict and cater to the needs, wants, and expectations of others, Jena tended to smother her true personality, thoughts and desires beneath her need to keep everyone who mattered to her happy. Well, no more.

"You're right," Justin responded as he opened the door. "I don't know you. But whose fault is that?"

Touché.

The inside of the facility had a much nicer, more

professional feel than the outside. In fact it looked and smelled like a real hospital. Jena's stress level eased a bit. Abbie's screams caught everyone's attention and the ten or so people in the waiting room to the right and the older woman at the registration desk straight ahead all stared at them.

"Hey, handsome," the woman behind the desk said, looking past Jena to Justin with a warm smile. "What are you bringing us tonight? Out of uniform?"

"Hi, Gayle," Justin said. "This is my…" Justin stopped. "Uh…my…"

Gayle lowered her head and peered up at him over the top rim of her eyeglasses.

Jena wanted to help him out but found herself at a loss regarding how to best describe their relationship. Was she his friend? Not really. In truth they barely knew each other. His lover? Did one drunken sexual encounter make them lovers? A woman he hardly knew who just happened to be the mother of the children he didn't know about and doesn't want? Bingo!

Jena decided to go with friend. "I'm a friend of Justin's." She reached out her hand to shake Gayle's and sat down in the chair facing her desk. "This is my daughter, Abbie." She removed the hat. "She's six weeks old and has been screaming like this for going on an hour and a half. She doesn't feel like she has a fever but her abdomen is mildly distended and firm. She's refusing her bottle and," she glanced up at Justin, "we felt it best she be examined by a doctor to make sure nothing serious is going on."

Gayle typed on her computer keyboard. "Insurance card."

"I…don't have insurance," Jena admitted, leaning

in to whisper. "But if you'd agree to a payment plan I promise to pay off the entire bill."

Gayle's expression all but branded Jena a liar. Then she shifted her disapproving gaze up to Justin no longer happy to see him.

"She's my daughter," he said boldly. "I'll make sure the bill is paid."

Gayle couldn't have looked more shocked if someone had slapped her across the face with a fish. But she regrouped and handed Jena a clipboard with papers to be filled out and a pen. If only a pitying look hadn't accompanied them.

Jena lowered her eyes and let out a breath. Her face burned with the heat of embarrassment. She hated being in this position. "Thank you," she said quietly. Then balancing Abbie against her chest with her left hand, she completed the necessary paperwork with her right.

After reviewing the forms Gayle studied Jena's face. "You're one of the Piermont twins?" she asked, with reverse snobbery.

Why, because Jena hadn't had time to put herself together for public viewing? Because a Piermont shouldn't need a payment plan? Because she didn't belong in their little urgent care center? Or with Justin?

"Not a word," Justin cautioned Gayle.

Like a man who didn't want people knowing he was in any way associated with her. Or that he'd fathered a baby. Two babies. Well, who needed him? "You found me out," Jena said with a forced laugh. She sat up a bit straighter and lifted her chin. She could do regal better than just about anyone when she needed to. "See. No worries you won't get paid. I'm a millionairess." With no currently available millions.

"Shshsh," she whispered to Abbie, hugging her close. "You're going to be fine." She and her sister and their mother would all be fine. After Abbie stopped crying, after Jena's surgery and after she found a way to meet the terms of her trust fund.

A payment plan. Justin followed Jena down the long hallway to one of the exam rooms reserved specifically for infants. It absolutely defied logic that Jena Piermont, whose family made The Forbes 400, a listing of the richest people in America, year after year, requested a payment plan for a bill that, at the most, might reach two hundred dollars. And she had no insurance? Doctor and hospital bills for her treatment during pregnancy and the delivery of two babies must have been considerable. But enough to drain her multi-million-dollar bank account?

No. More likely she'd squandered it on fancy clothes, fancy food, and a fancy lifestyle she obviously couldn't afford.

"Thanks, Mary," he said to the nurse manager who'd walked them to the room.

"I hear congratulations are in order," she whispered as he walked past her through the doorway.

"Tell Gayle not to expect any more specialty coffee deliveries while I'm out on patrol."

Mary smiled.

"If you wanted to keep Abbie and me your dirty little secret," Jena snapped, "why did you bring us someplace where you obviously know people?" She laid Abbie down on the paper-lined exam table and began to undress her.

Because he'd been thinking of his daughter, of getting her the best and quickest medical care available. Since he visited the urgent care center regularly in the course of his work and provided their evening security guards through his side business, he knew they'd take him in immediately. And despite Gayle's big mouth among the staff, he trusted their discretion when it came to outsiders.

Mary placed a disposable liner on the baby scale and Jena picked up Abbie and placed her on the scale like a pro. Justin took the first opportunity to really examine the baby he'd helped to create. Ten tiny fingers opening then closing into fists. Ten tiny toes attached to the most adorable little feet. A round head with baby-fine wisps of blonde hair. An innie belly button. A cutie pie.

Jena reported an uneventful pregnancy. Justin was happy to hear that. She took the thermometer probe from Mary, placed the tip in Abbie's armpit and held her arm to her side.

"You a nurse?" Mary asked Jena. Who nodded.

As far as he knew the only nursing she'd done was taking care of her mother who'd been physically and mentally disabled as a result of a traumatic brain injury. When she'd died a few years ago, Jena took on the role of social secretary to her jerk of a brother.

"But right now I'm more nervous first-time mom than nurse," Jena continued. "So don't assume I know anything."

"Got it," Mary said. "I have two of my own." The thermometer beeped.

"No fever," Mary said. "Any allergies?"

"Not that I know of." Jena picked up Abbie, held her naked body to her chest, and covered her with a pink knit baby blanket. While swaying from side to side she rattled off brand of formula, feeding amounts/ frequency/tolerance, and bowel habits. All stuff a father should know, so Justin paid close attention.

"I'll get Dr. Morloni in here as soon as I can," Mary said.

"Thanks." Justin opened the door for her. "Not that I'm not happy to see you, but what are you doing here so late?"

"Denise quit. At least tonight I have help. Tomorrow and Sunday I'm on all alone. You know any nurses looking for work?"

"What hours?" Jena asked.

"Four p.m. to twelve a.m. Why? You interested?"

"If I can work off my bill for this visit," Jena answered.

At the same time Justin blurted out, "No she is not interested. She's the mother of six-week-old twins. She needs to be home to take care of them."

For a split second Jena flashed Jaci's defiant don't-you-dare-tell-me-what-to-do look and he waited for her temper to flare.

Mary looked up at him. "Oh, boy."

She must have seen it too.

But Jena's expression quickly turned neutral and rather than yell, she remained composed and calmly said, "My decision to work or not to work is one in which you have no say. And whether I care for the twins myself or arrange for someone to care for them in my absence, I won't ever request or expect any assistance from you. So rest assured. My returning to town and returning to work will in no way impact your life. Feel free to carry on as if we don't exist."

Wow. A few well-chosen words really could sting as much as a slap across the face.

"You're an idiot," Mary said to him. Jena got a smile and a, "We'll talk before you leave, hon. Look," she pointed at Abbie who lay fast asleep in her mother's arms.

Jena cupped Abbie's head, closed her eyes and let out a relieved breath.

"Sit," Mary whispered. "Might as well have the doctor take a quick look since you're already here."

"I'm afraid if I move she'll start to cry again." Jena gave Mary a beautiful smile that up until that point he would have bet a week's wages she wasn't capable of.

Once alone Justin spoke quietly, so as not to wake Abbie. "I didn't mean to come off like you needed to stay with the babies twenty-four seven because I don't want anything to do with them." It was more about his daughters not being shuffled around between caregivers like he'd been. About them being able to sleep in their own beds and wake up in familiar surroundings. About them having a space that belonged to them where they felt safe and loved and welcome. "I don't know the first thing about how to care for them. But I'll do what I can to help." Although children had never been part of his plan for the future, now that he had them, he would damn well do a better job at fathering than his father had.

"Wow. You're full of surprises." Jena gave him a small half-smile. "I thought for sure you'd demand a paternity test to try to prove they weren't yours."

He laughed. Tried to keep quiet but couldn't help himself. "Honey, if you were intentionally trying to trap a guy into marriage, you'd have shot a hell of a lot higher than me."

Seems he couldn't say anything right tonight because she sucked in an affronted breath and took on a look of total outrage at his comment. "I would never, ever do such a thing."

"Shshsh," he reminded her to keep her voice down.

"What a horrible thing to imply," she whispered as loud as one could whisper.

"Women do it all the time." Just happened to one of his buddies down at the precinct, as a matter of fact.

"Well this one doesn't."

Of course she didn't. Protection had been his responsibility and he'd blown it. "No. You don't have to. You're beautiful and rich." What she lacked in personality she more than made up for in sex appeal. "Guys must be lining up to marry you."

In what he recognized as another attempt at not letting him know what she was thinking, she looked away, but not before he caught a glimpse of sadness. "And that's the only reason men would want to marry me, because of my looks and my money."

Damn it. "That's not what I meant."

His phone rang. He looked at the screen, noting the caller and the time."I have to take this." He turned to face the wall and accepted the call. "I'm sorry," he said to his pal Ryan. "I got tied up." And forgot all about their Friday night poker game. He never missed that game, looked forward to hanging out with the guys. Already Jena and the babies were screwing with his life.

"Damn it, man," Ryan said. "It was your turn to bring the beer."

Jena spoke up from behind him, "You know I don't think you're supposed to use a cell phone in here."

Ryan heard her. "No way, dude. Tell me you did not blow us off for some woman. First rule of poker night—"

"I know, I know. Never let a woman interfere with the game," Justin finished for him. Then he lowered his voice and added, "What about two women?" After all, Abbie was there, too.

"You go, bro," Ryan said, like Justin knew he would. "Call me later with the brag bits."

Not likely.

He ended the call and turned around to find Jena glaring at him. "Very nice," Jena said her words weighted down with sarcasm. "Don't think I don't know what you were inferring. And in the presence of your child."

Who was all of six weeks old.

The doc knocked and walked in.

Thank you.

"Hello, Justin." He shook Justin's hand. "And who do we have here?"

"My daughter." It came out a little easier that time. "She's six weeks old." Although he couldn't take credit for anything more than having strong, determined swimmers, he actually felt kind of proud to have fathered such a perfect baby. Two of them, since he assumed Annie was identical.

"If she grows up to look anything like her mother you'd better keep a loaded shotgun handy at all times."

For sure. And he'd aim it at any man who looked at the twins like Dr. Charmer—the staff's nickname for him—was looking at Jena. A ripple of possessiveness surprised him and he imagined aiming that shotgun at Dr. C.

Jena smiled sweetly, totally taken in by the man's spiel. "There are actually two of them. Abbie's twin sister is at home with my twin sister."

"Twin girls." He patted Justin on the shoulder. "Better you than me." He turned to Jena. "What brought you here tonight?"

As Jena recounted Abbie's medical history and the events leading up to their visit, Justin watched her, determined to learn the differences between her and Jaci. Right away he noted Jena was softer, more feminine and well-spoken. Proper. And, apparently easily taken in by a handsome, sweet-talking male as she hung dreamily on every word Dr. Charmer uttered. "It's none of your business what's going on between us," Justin intervened, feeling unusually territorial. Jena was the mother of his children. And he'd be damned if he would stand by and watch her fall prey to some hound dog doctor, or allow any other male a spot in his daughters' lives. They were his.

Life had just gotten infinitely more complicated.

"Just making small talk," Dr. Charmer said finally getting down to the exam. If nothing else, the nurses all agreed he was an excellent doctor with a superior—albeit a bit flirty—bedside manner.

Abbie did not like Dr. Charmer's stethoscope in contact with her skin or his fingers pressing on her belly or having a scope shoved in her ears and she screamed in protest.

Granted, Justin was no doctor, but based on what he could see and hear: Lungs: healthy. Vocal cords: working fine Temper: check plus.

Tough stuff, like her namesake, and his Grandma Abbie would have loved her at first glance. Justin had a sudden urge to hold his daughter and protect her from the man upsetting her, like a dad should.

Probably better to wait until she had some clothes on.

"She looks good," Dr. Charmer said. "You can get her dressed."

"Would you hand me the diaper bag?" Jena asked Justin.

He placed it on the head of the exam table.

Jena took out what she needed.

"Her ears look fine," Dr. Charmer said. "Her lungs are clear. She has good bowel sounds. No abdominal tenderness. No visible injuries. She's moving her extremities freely. If I had to guess, I'd say she had a bout of gas. If it happens again, it may be colic. Talk to your pediatrician."

"Can you recommend a good one?" Jena asked. "I've done some inquiring but haven't decided who to use. Two more weeks and the girls will need their next round of immunizations."

"You know in addition to urgent care cases we handle routine pediatrics by appointment, if you're interested."

She wouldn't be. The urgent care center wasn't near upscale enough for Jena.

"That'd be great," she said with a smile brighter than any he'd ever seen on Jaci. "Would it be okay if I requested you?"

No. Dr. Blake was a much better choice. Portly, married, Dr. Blake.

"I'd be insulted if you didn't."

He was going to be a lot more than insulted when Justin got finished with him.

What the heck was happening? Jena was the quiet one. The mousey one. The stuck up one. People didn't like her. Yet Mary did. And Dr. Charmer did—to the point Justin felt it necessary to attend every pediatric appointment from today on to prevent Jena from falling victim to his charm.

With Abbie diapered and dressed, Jena struggled to hold her and pour water into a bottle.

"I can hold her," Justin offered.

"It's okay," Jena said, taking a can of formula out of the diaper bag.

"I want to." She was his daughter and a good father would want to hold her.

Jena looked up at him. "Thank you," she said. "For not questioning if I was sure they were yours. For taking this much better than I'd thought you would."

Frankly he still felt sort of numb. But one thing he knew for certain, he'd do right by his girls.

Jena placed Abbie in his arms. So small. Delicate. He felt awkward, his hands too rough, too big.

"Hold her head." Jena positioned his hands where they needed to be then measured the formula powder and dumped it into the bottle. "I need a microwave."

"Down the hall to the right, third door on your left will be the staff break room."

Alone with his crying daughter for the first time the responsibility of parenthood hit him. What did he know about being a father? To girls, no less. About feeding them and dressing them and getting them to stop crying? Absolutely nothing. He swayed and rubbed Abbie's back the same way he'd watched Jena do it. "Daddy's got you while mommy's heating up your bottle."

Daddy and mommy. One of each. How he'd wished for a real mommy of his own when he'd been little. Grandma Abbie had tried. But she'd been old and tired. To be honest, he'd wished for a real daddy of his own, too. One who showed an interest in his kid by visiting his classroom on career day and attending baseball practices and games. One who took his kid out to dinner and enjoyed spending time with him instead of constantly looking for places to dump him so he could entertain women too numerous to remember any one in particular without interruption.

Jena returned. "Mary said they don't have anyone waiting for the room so we can take as long as we like."

He looked at the bottle and saw his hand reaching for it.

"You don't have to—"

Something strange happened. The man who had never before felt an inclination to hold or feed or have any contact with a baby said, "I want to," be the one to get his daughter to stop crying, which feeding her at this moment would hopefully do.

"Okay. Sit down." He did and Jena repositioned Abbie in his arms. "Keep her head elevated." He touched the nipple to Abbie's lips and she latched onto it like she hadn't eaten in weeks.

They both stared at their daughter, her eyes closed, the slurping of her contentedly sucking the only sound in the quiet room. It was a moment he'd never forget. And an opportunity to ask a question that'd been gnawing away at him since the morning he'd learned he'd slept with Jena not Jaci. "Why did you do it?" He looked up at Jena who'd taken a seat on the exam table. "Why did you have sex with me knowing I thought you were Jaci?"

Jena hopped off the exam table and walked over to the small sink. Her back to him she said, "I had a bit of a...fascination with you back in high school."

The surprises of the evening just kept on coming.

She opened a drawer and looked inside. "I joined the astronomy club because of it." She glanced over her shoulder and smiled. "So daddy would buy me a high-powered telescope."

She closed one drawer and opened another. "Did you know with the assistance of said high-powered tele-scope it was possible to see from the walk-in attic in the new wing of our house directly down the hill into your bedroom at your dad's house?"

He smiled. No he did not know that. "So you and Jaci—"

She whipped around. "Not Jaci. Only me. She didn't know. I swear."

Did she think he was mad? Actually, it kind of turned him on to think of her watching him in his bedroom.

She played with a Band-Aid wrapper. "You did a lot more studying than you let on in school."

Because no one gave his dad a free ride so he shouldn't expect one. Funny how that memory pre-sented itself in his dad's booming voice.

"You need to burp her." Jena came over, spread a cloth on his shoulder and showed him what to do. He breathed in her scent, similar to Jaci but more floral and fresh. He made a mental note of the difference.

"I did a lot more than study in that room and you know it." He watched her reaction to that statement and sure enough she started to look away, but not before he caught the tinge of deep pink on her pale cheeks. "You voyeur," he teased.

She didn't apologize or try to explain. "You looked gentle, like you truly cared for each one of them. Sometimes you lit candles."

Whatever it took to get the girl of the moment into his bed.

"Before we'd met up at the bar, I'd had a terrible fight with my brother over him pressuring me to marry a man I didn't know and had heard terrible things about."

Abbie must have sensed his tension because she started to fret. Or maybe it was the burp that followed that'd riled her up. "Good, girl," Jena said. "Now you can give her some more of the bottle." He got Abbie set up to finish the bottle on his own. And felt a bit proud of that, as stupid as it may seem.

"Anyway," Jena went on. "When the bartender told me to take you home the first thing that popped into my mind wasn't 'Ooooh goodie, now's my chance to get him into bed.' I wanted to get you home safely. And I figured I'd have a better chance of you coming with me thinking I was Jaci than knowing I was Jena."

She had that right. "You made the first move," Justin pointed out. For what reason he had no idea, just he felt it needed to be said.

"I know." She did not look at all repentant. "In your condo, you and me alone, I remembered how good it'd felt to have your hands on me down at the lake. I wanted that again. I wanted more. With you. I didn't want to lose my virginity to a man I had no feelings for, one who would only be marrying me for my trust fund. I wanted to share the experience with you."

Because she'd seen him treat other women gently. Yet he'd been too drunk to notice her inexperience or have a care with her untried body or even protect her. If Abbie wasn't in his arms he'd have banged his head against the wall until he achieved a level of pain he deserved. Or went unconscious. Whichever came first.

"Anyway," she shrugged. "It's done. And the next time will be better because I'll know what to expect and hopefully the man I'm with will be telling *me* how special *I* am and how good *I* feel."

Justin had spent so much time wondering why she'd done the switcheroo he'd never considered what it must have been like for her. "I'm sorry."

"Oh, it's not your fault," Jena said.

Then her words registered. "Next time it will be better." "When you say 'next time it will be better' does that mean you haven't been with anyone since me?"

Jena plucked a wooden tongue depressor from a canister on the counter by the sink and tapped it on her palm. "Turns out morning and evening sickness, exhaustion and maneuvering around with a big, fat pregnant belly didn't put me in much of a mood to go looking for love. Therefore, as of this moment, you remain my one and only," she said.

It shouldn't matter, but he kind of liked being her one and only.

CHAPTER THREE

JENA ended her call to Jaci and looked over at Justin in the driver's seat. He'd been quiet since they'd left the urgent care center. Introspective. "Jaci said Annie's sound asleep."

Justin stared straight ahead at the road. "Mm mm."

"Since Abbie's sound asleep, too, I was wondering if you'd do me a favor?"

He glanced her way. "Depends on what it is."

"I need to stop by the house." Since Mary had hired her on the spot and she'd be starting work the next afternoon, "I need to pick up the nursing uniforms I wore while taking care of my mom." Since she'd given back the maternity ones she'd borrowed down in South Carolina.

"Is it even legal for you to start work so quick?" he asked. "Mary could not have checked your references at eight o'clock on a Friday night. Do you even have experience in pediatrics?"

"Wow. Someone's grumpy." But he did turn in the direction of the estate.

"Abbie screamed for hours tonight," he continued. "What's going to happen if she does it again tomorrow night? And her mother isn't there to take care of her?"

"It's not like I plan to leave her home alone, for heav-

en's sake. Have a little faith in me, will you? Before I
accepted the job I called Jaci to make sure she was willing to watch the girls. And if there's a problem she'll
bring them to the urgent care center, like we did tonight,
and I'll be waiting, with a doctor, to take care of them."

"If you need money—"

This wasn't about money as much as it was about cre-
ating the need for Jaci to take care of the twins, without
Jena around, for more than an hour or two. An opportunity to put Jena's mind at ease, to confirm that Jaci
was, in fact, the right person to entrust with her precious
girls. Just in case... And Jena was running out of time.

But, "If I need money I'll work for it, thank you very
much." And get paid for it, in an actual paycheck which
she would put in her personal bank account which she
had sole control over. "And for your information, Mary
most certainly did check my references on a Friday
night. I gave her the home numbers for the doctor who
visited mom at home while I cared for her, for six years,
and for the family practice MD I worked part time for
while I was down in South Carolina. Both gave me very
high recommendations because even though you seem
to think very little of me, I am a hard worker and an
excellent nurse." Now he'd gone and made *her* crabby.
She stared out the window at the darkened street where
she used to ride her bike as a child.

Justin turned up the long drive, slowing when the
guard walked out of his little guardhouse. "You think
there's still a picture of me with orders to shoot on
sight?" he joked.

"Let's hope not."

Thank goodness she recognized the man on duty.

Justin lowered his window. The guard scowled. Jena

leaned toward him so he could see her. Her hand in contact with Justin's muscled thigh—for support, her back resting against Justin's chest—for balance, her nose inhaling Justin's arousing male scent—for the pure enjoyment of it... Oh, right, "Hi, Mitch. It's me. Jena."

He smiled. "Welcome home, Miss. Is Mr. Piermont expecting you?"

Shoot. "He's home? On a Friday night?" She considered asking Justin to turn around.

Mitch nodded. "I'll have to announce you."

She gave him her sweetest smile. "Would you mind announcing me after we're through the gate?"

He hesitated then smiled back. "Only for you, Miss." It paid to be nice and generous to one's employees.

Justin started to drive. "Why do you have to be announced in your own house? Why have you been staying with Jaci? What aren't you telling me?"

The stately white mansion and grand columns looked spectacular all lit up at night. And to the right, mom's pride and joy, bed after bed of colorful perennials, accented by huge, expertly carved and maintained topiaries, spotlighted, still magnificent, the highlight of the perfectly manicured grounds. So many happy childhood memories. Until her mother's breast cancer had invaded their perfect lives. Chemotherapy. Radiation. Hair loss. Weakness. Nausea. Vomiting. Bilateral mastectomies.

Mom and dad's relationship changed after that. Mom changed. Life changed.

The heat of Justin's large, warm hand on her thigh brought her back to the present. "You okay?"

She nodded. "Reminiscing." To avoid thinking about Jerald's temper. While he'd never raised a hand to Jena in anger, he had to Jaci. Many times, because she stood

up to him. Defied him. Like Jena had done, for the first
time, when she'd left town, and again at Jaci's benefit
two weeks ago.

They hadn't spoken since.

Justin steered around the final curve, the headlights
illuminating Jerald, standing on the front porch, waiting for her.

Bringing Justin had been a mistake bound to make
the entire situation worse. Jena covered his hand with
hers. "Please stay in the car."

"Your hand is like ice." He slammed on the brakes
about twenty feet from the porch and turned to face her.
"What's going on?"

"I'm not one of his favorite people at the moment."
And Jerald in a rage was a frightening sight indeed.
"Maybe I should come back tomorrow." When Jerald
was at work.

An abrupt knock on the window made her jump.
Heart pounding she turned to see Jerald looking back
at her. He tried to open her door. Thank goodness it
was locked.

Justin lowered her window halfway.

"It's about time you came to your senses," Jerald
said, trying the door again. "This house is where you
and your daughters belong. I had the room next to yours
made into a nursery."

A total turnaround from his "I'm through with both
of you" declaration to her and Jaci as he'd stormed off
after their last encounter. Jerald could be so nice and
accommodating. In order to achieve his desired objec-
tive, she reminded herself, which in this case was to get
Jena back into the family home, back under his con-

trol so he could continue his quest to barter her future
and her fortune for the benefit of Piermont Enterprises.

"Rather presumptuous of you, Jerry," Justin said,
calling Jerald by the nickname he hated.

At the sound of Justin's voice Jerald went rigid.
Slowly he bent to look through her window into the
driver's seat.

Justin gave him a goofy smile and waved.

"What the hell is he doing here?" Jerald yelled.

Friendly welcome over.

Abbie let out an unhappy whine at the noise.

Jena unlocked the door and got out. "Keep your voice
down," she said to Jerald, pulling him away from the
open window.

"Yeah, keep your voice down," Justin added, getting
out of the car. "My daughter is sleeping."

"You promised to stay in the car," Jena reminded
him.

"I did not," Justin said. "So how've you been, Jerry?"
he asked, enraging Jerald further.

"You and your spawn are not welcome on my property," Jerald blustered. "Leave now or I'll call security
and have you forcibly removed." He put his arm around
Jena and held her to his side.

"Stop it." Jena twisted away. "She's my daughter, too,
and has just as much right to be here as I do. This is the
Piermont estate. It's on Piermont property. And whether
you're happy with me or not, I'm still a Piermont."

"Him?" Jerald said, sounding like the remnants of
something foul coated his tongue. "That degenerate is
the twins' father? Have you completely lost your mind?
He ruined your sister's reputation."

Technically, Jaci had ruined her own reputation back in high school.

"Here I thought I was the last to know the girls were mine," Justin said, amused.

"Be quiet." Jena glared at him, hoping he got the full effect of her displeasure despite her being in the shadows.

"It wasn't enough to corrupt Jaci and destroy her chances for a respectable marriage. You had to go after Jena, too," Jerald accused. Then he turned to Jena, softened his tone and said, "Honey, I warned you about men like him, men who will do anything to snag themselves a Piermont," pretending to be a concerned big brother.

"It's not like that," Jena defended Justin, praying he didn't share the circumstances of their night together. The humiliation of Jerald knowing would be too much.

"Don't be a fool, Jena," Jerald said. "What happened to your insisting you wouldn't marry without love?"

That'd been her silly hope, an unrealistic dream.

"Men like him don't know how to love," Jerald went on. "He'll tell you what you want to hear to get what he wants. He'll marry you but he won't be faithful."

"Hey, wait a minute," Justin piped up.

"He'll sneak around," Jerald said. "But the wife always finds out. You have a soft heart, Jena. He'll hurt you. You'll be miserable married to a man like him."

"You can save your arguments," she said to Jerald. "He doesn't want to marry me."

"I'm standing right here, you know," Justin said. "And I'm capable of speaking for myself."

"So speak," Jerald challenged. "Profess your undying love. Make an offer of marriage. Go ahead. We're waiting."

Jerald should consider himself lucky Jena didn't see anything within reach she could use to clobber him over the head. Justin wanting to marry her, no matter how misguided his reasoning, would only further complicate her already complicated life.

Thank goodness Justin had the good sense to keep quiet.

"Just as I thought," Jerald said and turned to Jena. "I've been in contact with Thomas Rosendale's father. You remember Thomas?"

Her lab partner in AP Physics. Graduated second in their class. "I thought he was gay."

Jerald hopped right over the question of Thomas's sexual preference and said, "He needs a wife. He's up for partner in a prominent law firm on Madison Avenue. He owns a three bedroom on the Upper East Side. He's very successful and polite. He'd make a good husband. His father assured me Thomas would do his best to make you happy, and he'll adopt the twins and raise them as if they were his own."

"Over my dead body," Justin yelled.

"That can be arranged," Jerald taunted. "What do you say?" he asked Jena. "Will you at least think about it? Please?"

"No she will not think about it," Justin snapped.

Only because she had other more pressing matters to deal with first. But, "Please?" She looked Jerald in the eyes. "For years you have been trying to force the most horrible men on me," she said. "You accepted invitations, on my behalf, for dates I did *not* want to go on, with men you should have been protecting me from rather than pushing me to be seen with in public. When that didn't work to marry me off you used your position as my business manager to deny me access to my money. When I left you stopped paying my credit card bills and cancelled my company health insurance in an effort to make me come home. The hospital where the girls were born is threatening to put me into collection, for heaven's sake. And after all that, I finally get a please? Why are you asking so nicely? What's so special about Thomas? What's in it for you?"

"I didn't know you were pregnant," Jerald said. "If you'd have called me—"

"You could have called *me*," Justin said. "You *should* have called me. You don't need to bow down to your brother and marry when you don't want to. I have money saved up. When we get home—"

Jerald let out a condescending laugh. "How sweet. He has some money saved up," he mocked.

"Stop it," Jena said. It *was* sweet.

"She doesn't need whatever paltry sum you've amassed working as a minimum wage security guard. This is rich." Jerald laughed again. "He's pretending he has no idea how much you're worth once you marry."

"What's he talking about?" Justin asked.

"You mean you really don't know?" Jena asked. "Jaci didn't tell you? Ian didn't mention it?"

"You've been home with my twin daughters for two weeks, living in the same building as me and I just found out about it tonight," Justin said. "I think it's safe to say Jaci and Ian don't feel it necessary to keep me in their loop."

"Don't believe him," Jerald spat. "He knows. It's not a secret. Why else do you think he slept with you? What'd he feed you, some lie about a broken condom? Did he even wear one?"

Justin charged around the car.

Jerald went into some ridiculous martial arts pose as if that would effectively ward off an attack by a six-foot-tall enraged cop.

Abbie cried out.

Justin stopped.

Jena ran the few steps to the car and opened the rear door. "It's okay," she whispered. Please don't start crying again. "Mommy's right here." Abbie blinked and stretched but closed her eyes and went back to sleep.

Thank you.

"Bring her inside," Jerald said, opening the rear door opposite her. "Where's the other one?"

"Home with Jaci. We're not staying. I'm here to pick up some of my things." She turned to Justin. "Watch Abbie, I'll be out in a few minutes."

"We'll come with you," he offered.

"No." It'd be quicker if she went herself, so she turned and ran up the marble steps into the grand foyer.

"You're not worthy of her," Jerald told Justin after Jena disappeared into the house.

No, he wasn't, but he and Jena shared two infant daughters. And tonight he'd learned enough about her to peak his interest, to make him curious about the girl who'd spied on him with a high-powered telescope, who'd crushed on him from afar and the woman who'd chosen him as her first lover, who'd given birth to his babies without asking for or expecting anything from him. The millionairess socialite who'd been manipulated and controlled by her brother for years, yet had the inner strength to escape him despite being cut off from her funds and having to take a part time job in a doctor's office, while pregnant with twins, to support herself.

"How much will it cost me to get rid of you?" Jerald asked.

"I'm not for sale, Jerry."

"All men like you have a price." He scrunched his face like a troll. "Name it."

Justin closed the car door as quietly as he could so their conversation wouldn't disturb Abbie. "You seem hell bent on lumping me in with some unsavory fellows, Jerry." He kept his tone light but made it a point to insert "Jerry" in as often as possible to piss off the pompous ass. "But I'm in a league all my own."

"Because you're so vile and disreputable no one wants to sink low enough in society's regard to join you."

Justin crossed his arms and nodded. "Not bad, Jerry. Sounds like someone's developed himself a sense of humor over the past few years." About damn time.

"Stay away from her."

"No can do." Justin walked over to Jerry, acting all casual and carefree like the bum Jerry thought him to be. "You see now that she's back I'm thinking one night in the sack wasn't near enough. And I plan to use my status as her babies' daddy to my full advantage." Jerry wasn't the only one who could taunt. "And a great big FYI,"—for your information. "My little security business is something I do on the side." To earn enough money to keep him in his luxury high rise. "My full time gig is police officer."

From Jerry's surprise he had no idea.

Good. "That's right," Justin said nonchalantly, kicking the toe of his boot against a clump of something lodged in the thick grass. "I've taken an oath to uphold the law." Which is the only reason Jerry wasn't lying in a bloody ball for the crap he'd put Jena through. "And first thing Monday morning I plan to make use of every investigative and legal resource at my disposal to find out what laws you've broken by denying your sister access to her money."

Jerry didn't flinch. But he swallowed.

Play time over. Now to seal the deal. "Notice I'm planning to hold off until Monday." He leaned in and lowered his voice. "Because I think this weekend is all the time I'll need to come to Jena's rescue and ease her financial burden. How do you think she'll show her appreciation? Huh, Jerry?" He elbowed Jerry in his stiff side then rubbed his palms together conniving style. "Maybe she'll give me the opportunity to knock her up with another set of twins. You think?" Take that you overbearing, condescending jerk.

Footsteps sounded behind them. Jena ran down the stairs, a stuffed medium-sized duffel bag in one hand and a cloth carryall in the other. "I'm done."

"Let me take that for you." Justin grabbed the duffel, which turned out to be heavier than it looked, a bit surprised she hadn't sought out a servant to carry it for her. With a few short hours in her presence, Justin had come the realization he'd made a few glaringly incorrect assumptions about Jaci's homebody, except when out in high society, not as shy as he'd thought twin.

"Hold on a minute," Jerry said. "I need to give you something." He speed-walked toward the porch. "Don't leave," he yelled over his shoulder.

Atta boy. Go fetch Jena the info needed to access her accounts so they could put all this talk of marriage and

Thomas what's-his-name behind them, so she wouldn't be in a position where she needed to take the job at the urgent care center and could stay home to take care of the twins. Where she belonged.

Jena looked up at him? "What was that about?"

Justin shrugged. "No idea." He carried her bag to the car and placed it on the backseat next to Abbie.

No sooner did he close the door then he spied Jerald, hurrying back in their direction, too high class to full out sprint, but moving as fast as possible without officially lowering himself to the point of actual running. "Here." He handed Jena an accordion file folder, panting from his exertion, although he tried to cover it up with an elegant cough. "It's all in here." He patted the folder now in Jena's hands. "Your most recent bank statements, your checkbook, and a snapshot of your investment portfolio from August. You may not remember, but you signed signature cards when you turned eighteen so you can write your own checks."

Jena clutched the folder to her chest, looking overwhelmed, relieved, and on the verge of tears. "Thank you," she said quietly.

"I'm happy to go over it with you and answer any questions," Jerry said actually pulling off a caring tone. But the only things he cared about were his company's bottom line and himself.

"Let's go." Justin put his arm around Jena's shoulders and guided her to the car. Before getting in she looked over at Jerry and said, "I'll think about Thomas."

Oh no she wouldn't.

"Thank you," Jerry said. "Come back any time, Jena." He glared at Justin. "You and my nieces are always welcome."

The ride back to the condo was a quiet one and Justin used the time to think. And come to the conclusion, if Jerry acted as Jena's business manager, paying all her bills and managing her money, there was the possibility she didn't know how to do either on her own, which would explain the uneasy tension emanating from her side of the car.

Jena spent the trip staring out the window, maintaining a tight grip on her financial data like someone might try to wrestle it from her at any moment. Which was kind of disconcerting since the only other person in the car capable of wrestling was him.

He parked in a guest spot close to the front door, turned off his SUV and shifted in his seat to face her. "You okay?"

She just sat there, gazing out the window, looking lost and in no apparent hurry to exit, her demeanor not that of someone he'd identify as okay. But she nodded in response to his question.

"I'm not sure if you're aware," he said. "But in addition to my undergraduate degree in criminal justice, I minored in finance. And I worked at my dad's investment firm every summer from the time I turned sixteen until I graduated college. I'd be happy to take a look at everything Jerry gave you and help you make sense of it," he offered, half on edge, waiting to see if she'd lash out at being insulted by him thinking she didn't know how to manage her money when she did.

Instead of a reply, she reached up to dab at the corner of her eye with her knuckle and Justin wanted to pull her into his arms and tell her everything would be okay. That she could count on him to help her and take care of her.

Whoa. That came out of nowhere. But there was something about her, a naiveté long worn off in the women he dated, that made him want to be the man to teach her and tend to her, placing him in unfamiliar territory.

"Thank you," she said, so softly he almost didn't hear her. She inhaled a deep breath, let it out then turned to look at him. Light from the outside fixtures reflected in her watery eyes. "It's not that I'm dumb or lazy. It's the way I grew up," Jena explained, lowering the folder to her lap.

"While Jaci fought for independence I was content to be taken care of. I chose to blindly trust Jerald to manage my money. I chose to leave rather than fight him for control. But I have worked from the age of thirteen, managing the house and as a nurse for my mom, even while I went to college. After she passed away, I took on the role of Jerald's social secretary full time. Yet I never received a formal paycheck. Jerald made sure there was cash in the safe in his office, and I took what I needed when I needed it. My credit card bills came to the house and he paid them when he paid all the other bills. If I had to go somewhere there was always a car and driver waiting to take me."

She looked down and fiddled with the elastic band holding the folder together. "And now I'm a twenty-four-year old mother of two who can plan a dinner party for fourteen with two hours' notice, coordinate an exquisite gala for five hundred on a strict budget, and manage a staff of thirty-six, half of whom only speak Spanish, but I can't drive, I have no idea how much money I have aside from the two hundred thirty-six dollars in the envelope in my dresser drawer, and I don't know the first thing about paying bills or writing checks."

Justin reached out to take her cool hand into his. He squeezed it. "I promise you, by the end of the weekend, you will have your bills sorted and paid, you will know how much money you have in the bank and in your investment accounts, and you will know how to write a check."

She peered up at him from the corner of her eyes. "And the driving?"

He smiled. "If we can't find the study guide for a driver's permit test online, I'll pick one up from the DMV"—Department of Motor Vehicles—"on Monday. As soon as you pass the test, I will personally teach you how to drive and you can use my SUV to take your road test."

She dropped her precious papers to the floor, lunged her upper body across the center console, and wrapped her arms around his neck. "Thank you," she kissed his cheek. "So much." She kissed him again.

Then they were kissing for real. Because he'd turned his head, intent on catching her lips with his. Success.

For a split second she stiffened and he thought she might pull away. Then she melted against him, opened for him, and before he knew what he was doing he'd dragged the rest of her onto his lap like some hormone-crazed teenager looking to get lucky in daddy's Dodge.

His eyes may still be working on identifying the differences between Jena and Jaci, but his body sure recognized Jena, and at that moment, was most interested in rekindling their naked acquaintance.

They came up for air, both breathing heavy. "I'm sorry." He wasn't. "I shouldn't have—"

"It's okay." She started to move away. He let her go but was not at all happy about it. "I guess I made the first move." She patted down her hair and readjusted her blouse. "Again."

He smiled. "Next time it's my turn to make the first move." In a room with a bed, when the babies were sound asleep and Ian was somewhere else and there was no chance they'd be interrupted. Then he'd wipe "fine" from her memory and replace it with amazing, unforgettable, stupendous. Never to be topped by any other man.

She looked away, like she often did when she didn't want him to know what she was thinking. "Can we not tell Jaci how inept I am at managing my life?" she changed the subject. "I'd rather she not know."

"You're not inept you're inexperienced." He reached out, gently took her chin in his hand, and turned her head to face him. "By Monday that will no longer be the case, because I have the next two mornings off, and I plan to spend them teaching you." Hopefully about more than her finances. "And on account of the major secrets your loving sister and my alleged best friend have kept from me, I'm kind of looking forward to having some secrets to keep from them. You got anymore?"

She nodded. "You know the rich, gooey, chocolate cake Jaci delivers to you on your birthday?"

"Of course I do." With milk chocolate ganache frosting, layers of the best buttercream mixture he'd ever tasted, and dark chocolate shavings on top. His mouth watered. "Every year since I turned fifteen."

Jena smiled sadly and nodded. "They weren't from Jaci, they were from me. And she didn't buy them at a bakery, I made them."

"You?" No way. That cake was pastry chef quality. "From scratch? Come on."

"I spent a lot of time at home. I made friends with the staff. They taught me things."

She stared back at him, confident, seeming to dare him to question her. Well wudda you know? "That explains why Jaci missed my last birthday. That little liar. I'm going to—"

She smacked the base of her palm to her forehead. "I forgot your birthday. I can't believe it. I'm so sorry."

He reached out to move a curl that'd fallen down close to her eye. "I'm guessing you had a lot going on at the time." Since she would have been around eight months pregnant.

She nodded.

He leaned back in his seat. "It's been quite an evening," he said, letting out a huge breath, feeling weighted down by all the revelations of the past few hours.

She stretched. "I'm exhausted." She angled her watch to catch a ray of light. "Annie should be up for a bottle soon. Then hopefully I can sleep for a few uninterrupted hours so I'm bright and cheery for my new job tomorrow."

"Wait a minute," Justin said. "You have your money back. You don't *need* to work."

"Maybe not, but I like working as a nurse. And I promised Mary I'd help her out this weekend. She needs me."

"Your daughters need you, too," Justin pointed out. If given the choice, didn't women *want* to stay home to take care of their babies?

"Relax," Jena said. "It's sixteen hours. It'll be good

for me to have some time away from the girls, to use my skills, and engage in professional conversation. I'm not in a position to commit to more hours right now. And if I come to an agreement with Thomas, I'll be moving into the city in the next two months anyway."

Thomas. They were back to her considering a marriage to Thomas. "What is this fixation with marriage? You. Jaci. Your brother. I don't get it."

"Keep your voice down," Jena whispered.

He froze, waited to see if he'd woken Abbie, and said a private thank you for blessed quiet.

"When my father died," Jena said, keeping her voice low, "Jaci and my inheritances went into a trust. To be distributed on our twenty-fifth birthday."

November twenty-eighth. In two and a half months.

"Typical of my dad, controlling tyrant that he was, he placed stipulations on the money." She looked up at him. "To receive it, Jaci and I have to be married and living with our respective spouses by our twenty-fifth birthday. To be sure we don't enter into a sham of a marriage, the payments are to be broken up over five years at five million dollars per year for each of us. If one of us doesn't marry by the age of twenty-five, we forfeit our portion of the trust and the money will be donated to charities designated by my father before his death. If we divorce or separate during the five year period, we forfeit any monies not yet paid."

Even dead that evil, arrogant menace managed to exert his power. "Twenty-five million dollars is a strong incentive to marry."

Jena nodded. "It's my daughters' legacy, their future. And I will do whatever it takes to see they get it."

"Even marry a gay guy?" slipped out before he could stop it.

"Trust me when I tell you, he is a million times better than most of the other men Jerald's tried to pair me off with."

The opportunistic bloodsucker. "What's his interest, anyway?"

"Fathers come to Jerald looking to make a good match for their wayward sons. Men come to him looking for a quick infusion of cash our trust would provide to bolster their failing business endeavors and dwindling bank accounts. Both promise Jerald favors or contracts or something that he wants." She shrugged and turned to look out the window. "Not exactly how I'd hoped to meet my future husband," she said sadly.

Damn it. "It's only for five years, right?" An idea started to form. A way to keep her from marrying someone else, to protect her from her brother and have her for himself, temporarily, to ensure his daughters' financial future and make sure he would be the one and only daddy in their lives.

She nodded, staring into the night.

"Hell, five years isn't all that long. I'll marry you."

CHAPTER FOUR

"I NEED a nurse out here," Gayle called out. Again. One hour into her first shift and Jena had been called to patient sign-in to triage more than a dozen patients. Thank goodness Jaci had dropped her off two hours early to meet with Mary, review policies and procedures, and familiarize herself with the facility before she'd officially started work.

"I'm on my way," Jena called out, freshening the paper liner on the exam table in room four and stuffing it and a disposable gown into the trashcan.

"Everything okay?" Mary, who was supposed to be supervising her closely, asked as she hurried in the opposite direction down the hallway.

"Fine. How's that little boy?" A three-year-old found unresponsive for an undetermined period of time, and rather than call an ambulance the older brother had scooped him up and run, barefoot, through a major intersection, to the urgent care center.

Mary shook her head and gave Jena a look that said "not good." Out loud she said, "We're doing all we can for him. Paramedics are finally on their way to transport him to the hospital." Forty-five minutes after they'd placed the call thanks to a train derailment with multiple casualties.

Jena entered the lobby to find a woman carrying a small child, holding a bloodied cloth over the left side of the toddler's face, the woman's blouse and the little girl's pink overalls stained red. "What happened?" she asked, taking a pair of latex gloves from her pocket and slipping them on.

"I turned my back for a minute." The mother started to cry. "I don't care if that coffee table has been in my mother-in-law's family for years. When I get home I am tossing it into the street."

"Let me take a look, sweetie," Jena said to the little girl, pushing aside a mass of black curls and lifting the cloth to take a peek at the injury, a rather large laceration to the left eyebrow area. But the cloth had adhered to the wound and Jena would need to moisten the area with saline to get a better look. "It seems to have stopped bleeding. Gayle will take your information and we'll get you into a room."

"My daughter has been waiting for almost an hour," a big brute of man bellowed from the standing-room-only waiting area. His nine-year-old daughter, who sat quietly, in no apparent distress, watching cartoons on the television, had fallen from her bike, while wearing a helmet, and denied hitting her head. No visible head trauma. Right wrist swelling and pain. Minor scrapes and bruises to the extremities. Stable.

"I'm sorry for the wait."

"That's what you said half an hour ago." He stood up and stormed toward her.

"Is there a problem here?" a deep voice asked from behind her. Justin's voice. Jena had never been so happy to hear it.

"Yeah there's a problem." The man didn't back down.

Justin came to a stop beside her, khaki pants covering his long legs, a navy blue polo shirt with Rangore Security embroidered in red letters on the left breast pocket, clinging to his muscled chest. His bare arms thick and powerful. His light scent enough to attract, to make her crave closeness.

Justin didn't suffer the paunch of an overindulgent lifestyle or the pallid, diminished physique of a seventy hour week white-collar workaholic. He was an imposing specimen of man, the personification of macho alpha male, the standard to which she compared all potential marriageable males. The reason she found some otherwise decent men lacking.

"Well look at you," Gayle's voice intruded. "What did we do to deserve the head honcho tonight?"

Jena didn't have time to question Justin's unexpected arrival or wait for an answer to Gayle's question because she heard a siren. "We have a critically ill patient in the back," she told Justin. "I think that's our ambulance." She looked out the glass front door. Shoot. "Whose red car is that?" Parked perpendicular to the entrance, blocking the ramp.

"Mine," the woman carrying the bloodied little girl said.

Justin held out his hand. "Either you move it or I will."

The woman handed Justin her keys. On his way out he did something to the double doors to make both remain open.

"I'm guessing if it were your child in respiratory distress you'd want the doctor to give her his full attention," Jena said to the irate father. "Even if that meant people had to wait while he did."

The man returned to his seat.

"We're doing the best we can," she told the patients and family members waiting. "I've spoken with each of you and as soon as the doctor is ready you'll be called in, the most acute cases first, then by order of arrival."

For as long as they took to get there, the paramedics were in and out in under ten minutes. After they'd gone, Jena, Mary, and Dr. Morloni met in the hallway. Jena held up her pad. "I'm not quite comfortable with the laptops yet. But this is what we've got waiting and the order I think they need to be seen."

Mary leaned in to look at her notes.

"Three-year-old, audible wheeze. Color within normal limits. No fever. Increased respiratory effort. Nine-month-old. One hundred and three point seven temperature. Mild lethargy. Two toddler lacerations, one eyebrow vs. coffee table, the other thumb vs. steak knife. Nine-year-old fall from bike with right wrist pain and swelling, wearing a helmet, no signs or symptoms of head injury and a very impatient father. Then the rest by order of arrival, three sore throats requesting strep tests. Two ear pain and pressure with fevers. Two seventeen-year-olds one with back the other with shoulder pain. A six-year-old with a pea or peas obstructing his left nostril, right nostril clear, no respiratory distress. And a four-year-old who may have swallowed a coin or coins from a bowl of change, no reports of GI distress."

Jena looked between the two of them. "To speed things up I've documented vital signs, chief complaints and past medical histories on each of them in the computer. I put the audible wheeze in room one to keep him calm and the nine-month-old fever in room two to get him out of the crowded waiting room."

"You done good," Dr. Morloni said. "We're back in business." Laptop in hand, he turned and walked in the direction of room one.

"These two." Mary pointed to the two seventeen-year-olds on Jena's list. "Did they come in with their parents?"

"An older gentleman who claims to be guardian to both."

"Insurance?"

"You'll have to check with Gayle, but I think he planned to pay cash."

Mary shook her head. "Point them out to Justin." When Jena looked up at her in question Mary added, "Local drug dealers send teenagers in to get prescriptions for narcotic pain medication which they turn around and sell on the streets."

"That's terrible."

Mary looked her in the eye. "Prepare to see a lot worse."

"May I ask a question?" Jena asked. "Unrelated to the patient population?"

"Fire away."

"What's Justin doing here?"

Mary smiled. "We contract with his company for evening security. This plaza is busy during the day, but we're all alone after five p.m." She removed her hairband and redid her pony tail. "Being able to advertise we have security on site at night helps us attract quality staff and expands our patient catchment area into the neighboring middle class towns."

"Does *he* usually work here?"

"On occasion, as his schedule at the police station allows. But I was told Steve would be on duty this weekend." She smiled. "I'm guessing the change has something to do with you."

Jena didn't know whether to be flattered that he'd shown up to spend time with her or insulted that he'd come to keep an eye on her because he didn't think her capable.

"Hey," Mary said, moving her head around to catch Jena's attention. "Dr. Morloni's right. You did a great job holding things together."

Jena smiled. "Thanks. Honestly, I enjoyed every crazy minute of it." For weeks her life revolved around caring for the twins. Jena loved being a mom. But her temporary job, which entailed three of her favorite activities, organizing, prioritizing, and nursing, energized and revitalized her.

After filling the rooms and walking the wrist injury to X-ray, Jena found Justin in the lobby. "May I speak with you?"

He followed her into the hallway.

"There are two teenagers in the waiting area, sitting with an older gentleman," she informed him, keeping her voice hushed.

"I noticed them."

"Both are here with complaints of pain and Mary asked me to point them out to you. Something about a drug dealer sending kids in to get prescriptions for narcotics."

"They fit the profile." Justin ran his fingers over his goatee. "Let Mary handle them."

Absolutely not. "I so appreciate your confidence in my skill as a nurse and my ability to handle this job." She turned to leave.

He caught her by the arm, his large hand strong, yet

gentle. "These are street kids," he whispered forcefully. "They're more dangerous than they look. Working in rural South Carolina give you a lot of experience dealing with patients who'd have no problem pulling a knife on you to get what they want?"

So he'd been pumping Jaci for more information about where she'd been. And no, it hadn't. A sudden chill made her twitch. But that did not lessen her resolve to do the job she'd come here to do. "If taking care of street kids, as you call them, is part of my job responsibilities, then best I learn how to deal with them. And if keeping me safe is part of your job responsibilities, best you focus on that rather than worrying about my past work experience."

"You're as stubborn as your sister."

Not quite, but she liked that he thought so.

"Okay," he acquiesced. "Take them in one at a time, and not until the doctor's ready for them. Make sure I'm in the lobby and I see you walk each one in."

She nodded her understanding.

"Anything makes you uncomfortable, you call me."

She looked up and saw his concern. "I will." Instead of feeling flattered or insulted by his presence her first night at work, she felt appreciative, realizing he'd come to keep her safe. "Thank you," she said, "for being here." Because it provided her a level of comfort she may not have had otherwise.

He skimmed his index finger down the side of her face. "You can be real sweet sometimes."

She winked, "When it suits me," and returned to work.

The next two hours went by in a blur of activity, but Jena still made time to call home twice to check on the girls, who were fine. Mary insisted on accompanying her for the discharge of each of the teens, which turned out to be a good thing as one in particular started arguing and begging when Dr. Morloni a.k.a. Dr. Charmer, informed the patient his exam was negative and recommended over the counter non-steroidal anti-inflammatory medication for pain management.

The boy's desperation clawed at Jena's heart, to be so young and possibly involved in the illegal drug trade. What would happen to him when the dealer found out he'd been unsuccessful?

"I tried," Justin said when he returned from escorting the boys and their "guardian" to Gayle to pay then to the parking lot to leave. "I gave each of them the chance to come clean, to give up the name of the drug dealer who put them up to coming in for narcotics prescriptions in return for police protection."

Great. Maybe...

He shook his head. "They laughed and shared their thoughts on police and their protection. I won't pollute your ears with the specifics. Suffice it to say they weren't interested."

Stupid. Maybe if they'd had access to a quality kids club with positive role models to look out for them when they were younger, or vocational training programs to funnel them into legal, well-paying jobs. Jena made a mental note to research what programs and services were available to the youth of the area. Jaci had championed women in crisis. Maybe with some of the money from her trust Jena could do the same for children.

"Hey." With a finger under her chin Justin nudged her face up to look at him. "You can't help people who don't want to be helped."

"Says the jaded cop."

"Not jaded as much as realistic." He smiled. "Your brother was right. You *do* have a soft heart."

"They're kids," Jena pointed out.

"In this area, childhood ends a lot younger than seventeen. Come on." He put his arm around her shoulders and guided her down the hall. "I heard Mary tell you to eat your dinner."

In the break room, Jena washed her hands in the small sink and Justin collected their bagged meals from the mini-fridge. Then Justin washed his hands and Jena poured two cups of coffee which she carried to the round four-person table in the corner.

In the process of unwrapping his deli sandwich Justin said, "Last night I promised you would have your bills sorted and paid, you would understand your investments and know how much money you had, and you'd be writing checks by Monday. That's not going to happen if tomorrow you refuse my calls and pretend you're not home when I knock on your door like you did today." He bit into half of what looked like a twelve inch Italian combo sub.

So he'd figured out the truth. Well, Jena had another bit of truth for him. "I'm not going to marry you," she blurted out. There. She said it. No more thinking about his degrading non-proposal. *"Hell, five years isn't all that long. I'll marry you."* Or how much his I-can-put-up-with-anything-for-five-years attitude bothered her. Like she was a nuisance. Someone to be tolerated.

Justin took his time chewing and didn't respond until after he swallowed. "Funny, I don't recall requiring marriage to help you with your finances." He casually reached for a creamer from the basket in the center of the table, poured it into his coffee and stirred. "But since you brought up the topic, why not?"

"You really want to get into this?" She entwined her fingers on the table. "Here. Now."

"No time like the present, don't you think?" He took another bite of his sandwich.

Jena had lost her appetite. This was her opportunity to tell him, to dispel any notion of them getting married. To reveal the truth. Soon she would no longer be an exact replica of Jaci and the only part of her he desired—her body—would be altered, her full womanly curves gone forever. Unless...no. She'd made her decision, would not change her mind. She opened her mouth. Closed it. Could not find the words, where to start, how to explain. She needed more time. Only she didn't have time. So she settled on, "It would never work," and busied herself by adding two creamers and a packet of sugar to her coffee so she didn't have to look at him.

"Why wouldn't it work?" He stuffed more food into his mouth.

So many reasons. For starters, "because each time we were intimate I'd know you'd rather be with my sister. That I'll never be anything more to you than a poor substitute for the woman you really want."

He choked.

Good.

"That's not true."

"You feel so good Jaci," Jena repeated the words he'd uttered over and over when they'd been in bed together. "Do you have any idea how special you are?"

"That's not fair." He placed his sandwich on the paper wrapper. "I said those things because I *thought* I was in bed with Jaci. Because you'd led me to *believe* I was in bed with Jaci."

"Which gave you the opportunity to pour out your true feelings."

"I was drunk."

"A drunk man's words are a sober man's thoughts."

"This is nuts." He slapped his hand on the table. "You won't marry me, the father of your daughters, because of a bit of wisdom you found inside a fortune cookie?"

"I won't marry you because you don't want to marry me." She pushed away from the table. "I won't marry you because making you a daily part of my daughters' lives, knowing you plan to desert all of us in five years is cruel." She stood. "I won't marry you because Jerald's right." She scooped up her uneaten dinner and turned to leave. "I'd be miserable married to a man like you." A man she would love who could never love her, one focused on physical beauty and incapable of monogamy. At least if she married Thomas terms could be negotiated, time frames agreed to, her heart protected. And her body wouldn't matter.

"Wait." Justin made it to the door before she could open it. "I *do* want to marry you."

"Why?" she asked, her blue eyes challenging him.

Because it was the right thing to do. The honorable thing. But from the look on her face he was pretty sure neither answer would satisfy her.

"Because I'm rich?" she asked. "Because if you marry me, you'll be rich too?"

No.

Before he could expand his no from an instantaneous mental reaction to an actual verbal response she said,

"Because I'm pretty?" She grazed her fingers down his chest enticingly. "Because you want my body night after night?"

Oh, yeah. He liked that idea. He turned them so her back was to the door and pressed his body to hers. "I don't need your money," he whispered in her ear. "And maybe five years will turn into ten or twenty or a life-time." He kissed down the side of her neck. "We won't know until we give marriage a try. But no matter what happens between us, I will never desert my daughters."

He kissed back up to her ear. "While we're figuring it all out, sex night after night sounds real good to me." He brought his hand to her breast. "And trust me." He caressed until he felt the tight bud of her nipple through her bra and blouse. "I'll make you feel so good so often you won't have time to be miserable."

He moved his lips to hers. Kissed her, tasted her, wanted more of her. "You have the most amazing breasts." He explored their supple fullness with both hands.

She pushed him away. "And what if I didn't?" she snapped, straightening her clothes. "What if I didn't have amazing breasts? What if my body repulsed you?"

She wasn't making any sense. "But it doesn't. It's perfect. I love your body. I want your body." Any man who swung toward heterosexual would want her body.

At that last thought, an unfamiliar, possessive, mine, mine, mine all mine popped into Justin's head.

Jena shoved him.

"What?"

"I am more than a pair of breasts." She had tears in her eyes. And he'd put them there. An odd, uncomfortable pressure settled in his chest.

She reached for the door.

He grabbed her hand. "What's wrong?" How had complimenting her body taken such a wrong turn?

"I can't do this," she said. "Please." She looked up at him. "I need to get back to work."

The aftermath of whatever the hell happened between them in the break room helped Justin recognize yet another difference between Jena and Jaci. The silent treatment. For better or for worse, Jaci put her emotions out there for all to see. In stark contrast to her sister, when something upset Jena, she went quiet. Of course she was too well-mannered to completely ignore him, but her interactions turned brief, coolly polite, and only when necessary.

She didn't want to marry him? Fine. He'd tried to do the right thing. She'd turned him down. Done. Pressure off. He could still parent without the hassle of marriage. Even better.

Jena smiled warmly at an unkempt woman in the waiting area, helped her with her diaper bag and, while accompanying her and a small child to an exam room, chatted like they were old friends. Comfortable. Genuine.

When she passed by Justin he may as well have been a cobweb for all the attention she paid him. They'd reverted back to high school.

Except now he couldn't help noticing *her*. Long blonde curls restrained in a tight bun, her luscious curves hidden beneath a boxy scrub top, and her face devoid of trendy, high-fashion makeup, she looked nothing like socialite Jena Piermont from the society pages of newspapers and magazines. She looked better. Real.

Desirable.

And he had a hankering for the genuine version of Jena.

Dr. Charmer passed her in the hallway and smiled.

Justin imagined the satisfying crack of dislocating the jaw attached to that smile with one powerful punch.

Which made no sense. Because Justin didn't do jealousy. Except, apparently where Jena, the mother of his twins was concerned, he did.

Lord help him.

A married couple returned to the desk to check out with Gayle. The man guided his wife with a gentle hand at her mid-back while holding their sleeping baby in a car seat. He'd watched them and listened to them since they'd arrived. They were about the same age as he and Jena, their baby a couple of months older than the twins. The woman had been nervous, worried about the child's fever and bright red cheeks. The man held her hand or sat with his arm around her while she rested her head on his shoulder.

The guy probably had a better role model growing up than Justin had. He didn't know how to be the type of man Jena wanted. The type of man she deserved. That didn't stop a small part of him from wondering what if?

Thank goodness work saved him from his thoughts. "You folks all set?" he asked as they stood. "I'll escort you out."

The man opened the car door for his wife then walked to the other side of the car and placed the car seat in its base.

"How long have you been married?" Justin asked.

"A few weeks," the man replied.

So they'd had the baby first, too.

"Thank you," the man said and got into the car. Before he started the engine, he leaned over to kiss his wife. She smiled at her husband like he was the most special man in the world.

He imagined Jena giving him a look like that and went all warm inside. Until he remembered women like Jena didn't give men like him looks like that. Because he didn't do love, sucked at demonstrating affection, and while she was looking for long term he'd never managed to stay with the same woman longer than one month. Twenty-two days to be exact. And the last three he'd spent ignoring her phone calls until she officially broke it off.

Back inside his cell phone buzzed. He checked the number—Jaci—and walked out of Gayle's hearing. "What's wrong?"

"Hello to you, too," Jaci said. "The girls are fine, sleeping like little angels."

He relaxed.

"Ian just told me you scheduled yourself to work at the urgent care center tonight. Very interesting," she teased.

"What do you want?" he asked.

"To know how Jena's doing. We haven't heard from her in over an hour." Despite the non-stop pace of patient after patient with little to no downtime in between, Jena had managed to check on the twins. Caring. Concerned. A good mother. Unlike his who'd chosen the lure of the Las Vegas stage over caring for a toddler. Without so much as a phone call or birthday card since.

"She's fine." He watched Jena move from one exam room to the next. Purposeful. Confident. Impressive. "Just busy."

"Ian also tells me you'll be giving her a ride home tonight to save him a trip out?"

"Yup." Justin picked up an abandoned tiny sneaker, lying on its side at the base of a potted plant and put it on the corner of Gayle's desk.

"I don't know," Jaci said. "She was pretty quiet today and didn't want to see you when you stopped by. Did something happen between the two of you last night?"

Interesting. So Jena hadn't shared his offer of marriage with her sister.

"Is she okay with you bringing her home?" Jaci asked.

She'd have to be since she'd have no other option. "Yup."

"Can you put her on? I'd like to hear it from her."

"Nope, she's in with a patient." That wasn't a lie.

"Have her call me."

"Sure thing." That was. "But don't worry if she doesn't. It's crazy here tonight."

The next time Jena went to breeze by him without a word he reached out to stop her. "Jaci called."

She stiffened and flashed him a worried glance.

"The babies are fine. She wanted you to know since they're asleep she's going to sleep," he lied.

"Thank you," she said without looking at him and continued on her way.

A few minutes before close, upon returning from investigating a disturbance behind the building, Justin met up with a worried Gayle hurrying toward him. "One of those boys you escorted out of here earlier came back."

Justin sped up.

"He said something to Jena and the fool girl followed him outside," Gayle said.

Justin broke into a run.

"I told her to wait for you," Gayle said as he passed her on his way to the entrance.

"If I'm not back in one minute call the police." Justin shot out into the dark. "Jena," he yelled.

Nothing.

"Jena," he yelled again, louder, so anyone within a mile radius would hear him.

Nothing.

So he listened. Cars driving past. A horn honked in the distance. Then quiet. A muffled... He turned to the right. Followed the sound to the far end of the parking lot where the spaces designated for the urgent care staff were located, noting it seemed darker and more shadowed than it had earlier. "If you hurt her I'll kill you," he called out. Even unarmed—because the urgent care center management did not want their security guards to carry weapons of any type with children around—he could do it. And would.

He looked up to see the corner parking lot light out.

How convenient.

He ran.

"Jena."

"I'm he—"

Someone cut off her response.

Not smart.

Justin followed her voice. Quietly. He crept between two cars to the grassy edge of the parking lot and saw her shadowed form, on the ground with someone on their knees behind her, a hand covering her mouth.

An uneasy feeling ran a chilly sprint up his spine.

Two teens accompanied by an elderly man had entered the care center earlier. He scanned the area and behind him for the other two.

Jena began to struggle.

The person behind her jerked an arm around her throat.

Justin's body tightened with rage. He would not allow that miscreant to hurt her, or worse, would not even entertain the possibility of his daughters growing up without their mom. And fueled by an emotion powerful enough to make him ignore proper police procedure and the good instincts that'd kept him safe over the years, Justin sprang to action. "Release her this second if you want to live." He showed himself and stalked toward the attacker who didn't move. "I can make it quick or I can make you die an excruciatingly slow and painful death."

Jena tried to fight, twisting, gasping...

"Don't—" Something struck the side of his head. A pipe? A bat? He held in a shout of pain. His vision blurred. Unable to stand he dropped and rolled onto his side, fought to remain conscious.

"Don't hurt him," Jena cried out. "What do you want?"

Money. Drugs. Her. Unacceptable. Justin struggled onto his knees, willed his head to stop spinning.

"Stay down," a male voice yelled.

Another male voice, this one sounding panicked said, "Let's go."

Jena crawled over to him. "Are you okay?" She gently touched the side of his head. "You're bleeding," she cried out.

He put his arm around her, would not let them touch her.

The two men loomed over them.

"I told you this wouldn't work," one of the men said. "If we show up—"

Justin chose their moment of conflict and inattention to jump—well stumble—to his feet and fight. His right fist connected with a nose, his elbow with a cheek. A siren sounded in the distance. Thank goodness because Justin felt seconds from collapsing to the ground.

The siren grew louder.

The men ran off. But Justin would make sure they were found.

He swayed. Jena caught him, maneuvered him up against the side of a minivan, and pressed her body to his to keep him upright.

"What the hell were you thinking?" he yelled and made his headache even worse in the process.

"He said when they showed up without the prescriptions the drug dealer beat up his friend and he was scared to come in for treatment because you'd banned them from ever coming back. I'm so sorry." She hugged him.

Damn she felt good. He reached down, grabbed her butt and pulled her hips flush with his.

She tilted her head up to him. "On account of you likely have a head injury I'm going to overlook this little display."

"I want you, Jena." He tried to nuzzle her ear, the movement throwing him off balance, tilting him forward.

"Now I know you're not thinking clearly," she joked, throwing her entire weight against him—which he liked a lot. "Stop moving around or I'm going to drop you."

A car screeched into the parking lot. A siren echoed in his head. Loud. Make it stop. He clutched his hands

over his ears. Lights blinded him. A car door slammed.
He groaned but knew enough to reach for his badge in
his front pocket and held it up. "Officer Justin Rangore.
MVPD. Two men. One lured Jena into the parking lot."

"One pretended to be injured. But once outside they
tried to convince me to get them narcotics," Jena explained. "Justin was working security. He came out to
find me and they hit him in the head. He needs to go
to the Emergency Room."

"They fled on foot," Justin added. "Heading north."

The officer conveyed the information into the radio
affixed to her shoulder. "That's a pretty nasty cut," she
noted.

Yeah. Cut. He wanted to cut with the chit chat and
take Jena to bed.

Someone said something, sounded far away.

"Stay with me." Jena's voice broke through the haze.

"I want to. I really do." Again. At his place. In his
bed. All night long. If he could just get rid of the pain
in his head. "Let's go home."

Of course she didn't let him go home until after he'd
had an X-ray, a CT scan, a tetanus shot, and twelve
stitches. None of which were all that bad since Jena
stayed with him, holding his hand, talking quietly, the
sweet melody of her voice relaxing him.

The best part of the entire night was the neurologist
informing Jena and Ian that Justin had a concussion and
would need to be woken up hourly until morning, and
Jena insisting since she was responsible for his injury
she be the one to do it.

After driving them home, Ian walked Justin up to
his condo while Jena went to check on the twins, give
Jaci an update and change out of her uniform.

Into something clingy and skimpy would be his preference.

"You going to be okay?" Ian asked. He'd been unusually quiet at the hospital, on the ride home, and in the elevator.

Justin plopped onto the couch. "Yeah. I promise I won't die." As soon as the words left his mouth Justin wanted to suck them back in. "Hey. I'm sorry." Because Ian had lost four of his buddies in the explosion that'd left him with a permanent limp. Damn war. "I didn't mean—"

"I know," Ian said. "You need help getting changed?"

"If I do I don't want it from you."

Ian smiled. "I guess that blow to the head hasn't affected your sex drive any."

If anything it'd made it even more powerful. Or maybe that'd been hours of close proximity to Jena.

"Take it easy on her," Ian warned. "Jaci's worried about Jena, says she hasn't been herself since her return."

Justin liked the changes.

"She's been preoccupied, quiet and secretive," Ian went on. "Jaci thinks it has something to do with Jerry the jerk."

"I'm taking care of it," was all he'd share. "Tell Jaci not to worry."

Ian stiffened, looking ready for battle. "What's going on?"

Justin yawned. "I'm taking care of it," he repeated, feeling himself drifting off to sleep.

Jena's voice woke him. "Help me get him up."

Justin smiled.

But those weren't Jena's dainty hands pushing into his armpits and lifting him to a standing position.

"Let's get him undressed," she said.

"Yeah. Let's," Justin said, liking the idea of getting naked with Jena. "I can walk." He twisted out of Ian's hold. "Three's a crowd. Good night, Ian." He lifted his shirt over his head, forgetting about his stiches. "Yowza," he yelled out when his collar rubbed along his sensitive suture line.

"Be careful." Jena took him by the arm. "Come on. I'll get you cleaned up and ready for bed."

"Call if you need me," Ian said, from behind them.

"I will," Jena said at the same time Justin said, "We won't." He had everything under control. Except for the dizziness. He leaned on Jena for balance. And the throbbing ache in his head. No chance a little headache, okay, a big headache, was going to keep him from having Jena. Again. Lots of agains.

CHAPTER FIVE

JENA led Justin into the bathroom, knowing his shirt was stained with blood and would have to be removed at some point, wishing he hadn't chosen to expose so much of his delectable body before she'd had a chance to fully prepare herself to combat the overwhelming desire to touch it. She closed the lid to the toilet. "Sit." He was a bit unsteady on his feet so she guided him down, which put his enticingly bare chest in full view, close enough to kiss.

Stop that, she chided herself for unprofessional thoughts. She was here as a nurse, nothing more.

Smooth skin covered exquisitely defined muscles. A dusting of hair up high and a line from his navel down...

He undid the top button of his slacks. "You like what you see?"

She most certainly did. What healthy, heterosexual woman wouldn't? "You've seen one you've seen them all," she said, belittling the fact men's naked bodies varied greatly in their aesthetic qualities. And Justin's earned a check plus in each box on her What I Like Most About Men's Bodies wish list.

He cleared his throat. "You going to clean up my head or is there another reason you brought me in here?"

He smiled a flirty all-you-have-to-do-is-ask smile, at least that's how she chose to interpret it.

"How are you feeling?" Jena asked to remind herself he'd been struck in the head a few hours earlier, had been diagnosed with a concussion and received twelve stiches. Only a callous, self-centered woman would entertain sexual thoughts while providing care to a man who'd been injured trying to protect her, a man who was in no shape, neurologically or physically, to engage in the totally inappropriate acts circulating through her mind.

Bad Jena.

"I'm a little tired." He smiled again. "But up for anything."

Okay. Conversation not helping. So she focused on his suture line instead. The ER doc had done a nice job of bringing the wound edges together, the stitches relatively equidistant and coated with antibiotic ointment. "I want to clean some of this blood out of your hair. Where are your washcloths?"

"Under the sink."

Jena retrieved a few and got to work. After a minute or two Justin sighed. "You have a very gentle touch."

She smiled. "Thank you."

"I didn't think I'd like this as much as I do," he said.

She looked down at him. "Like what?"

He opened his eyes. "You taking care of me."

She liked it, too.

At some point while she'd been concentrating on her task, rinsing and re-wetting the cloth, he'd shifted so now she stood between his spread thighs, his face pointed straight ahead at her breasts. She could almost feel his heated gaze. Her nipples went tingly and hard, the sensation divine. And one she would soon miss mightily. She fought back sorrow, needed to focus on the big picture. Life.

"You're killing me," he said.

Lost in thought she'd been too rough. "I'm sorry." She stopped rubbing his head and went to step back.

He palmed her waist and pulled her close, dropped his forehead to rest just above her belly. "You smell so good, look so good. I want to touch you, undress you. Take those tight, aroused nipples into my mouth."

Heaven help her she wanted the same things, especially to feel his mouth on her nipples. One last time.

"You have no idea what being this close to you is doing to me."

Oh yes she did, because it was doing the same to her.

"What would you do if I touched you? Would you let me?"

Yes.

As if he'd heard her mental response he set a gentle hand on her right breast, ran his thumb across its peak which sent a jolt of pure potent arousal raging through her system. Wonderful yet worrisome. Without sensitive, responsive nipples, would she ever again feel this overwhelmingly extraordinary desire for a man?

"You okay?" he asked.

"I'm fine." Not really. "But I think that whack to the head dislodged your impulse control." The condition apparently contagious as Jena had a few impulses on the verge of slipping outside of her control, too. The impulse to lift her shirt, grab him by the ears and direct his mouth to where she wanted it. The impulse to press her lips to his, to slip her tongue into his mouth and taste him, devour him. The impulse to straddle his lap and rub herself shamelessly along the length of the erection gaining prominence behind his zipper. Seems he was physically capable after all. But...

Think nurse-patient relationship. Nothing more. "Your head is clean enough." She tossed the washcloth into the sink. Distance would really help this situation. And sleep. "Where's your acetaminophen?"

He didn't answer.

She tried to step away. He held her close, not on board with the distance part of her plan. "Come on," she said.

Nothing.

"Justin?"

"Don't move," he said. A moment later he added, "I think I'm going to be sick."

And he was. Good thing she hadn't listened when he'd told her not to move. "That's two for two." When he was finished she handed him a clean dampened cloth to wash his face. "Two times in your condo during which you've had your hands on my body. Two times you drop to your knees and heave up the contents of your stomach as a result. Is it my perfume? My shampoo? Me?"

He sat on the floor, his back against the wall, looking miserable. "First time," he held up his index finger, "hangover. Second time," he added his middle finger, "concussion. It's not you."

Although tonight's injury and subsequent GI distress could be directly attributed to her stupidity in running out into the parking lot alone with someone Justin had told her to be cautious of.

He reached for the towel bar and started to pull himself up. "You think I like you seeing me at my worst?"

She rushed to help him. "Let me help you." She

tugged on his arm. But really he did most of the work himself. "You still nauseous?" If he vomited again she'd be on the phone, calling the doctor.

"I'm fine," he said not looking or sounding fine. "Let's go to bed."

Time to firm up the sleeping arrangements. "During your little impromptu nap a few minutes ago Ian said I could sleep in his bed."

"Did he have a big smile on his face when he said it?"

Come to think of it, yes.

"You're sleeping with *me*." He grabbed her hand and led her to his cave. Very me man you woman you do what man say.

A big apology to feminists worldwide, but she kind of liked it. Although, "It's a bad idea, Justin. We can't—"

"You promised the ER doc you'd keep an eye on me through the night."

Yes, she had.

"How are you going to do that when you're in another room?"

"I'll set the alarm on my phone. I'll come in to wake you every hour."

"Not good enough." He dragged her into his room without turning on the light. "The more I argue, the more my head hurts."

"Let me get you some—" Before she could name a pain reliever he said, "You're all I need."

How could a women argue with that?

He released her hand, unzipped his pants and let them fall to the floor. "Would you undo my shoes?"

Of course. That's the reason she was here. To take care of him. Caring for others is what Jena did best.

Naked except for a pair of cotton boxer briefs—

the room too dark for her to see anything more than the basic outline of his body, darn it all—he lifted the covers and slid into the middle of his queen-sized bed where he laid down on his side, held up the covers, and waited for her.

She removed her phone from the pocket of her lounge pants, pressed the buttons necessary to set the alarm for one hour, and placed it on the bedside table. Just for to-night. She climbed in beside him. Because of his head injury. She turned on her side facing away from him. Definitely not because she wanted to be there just as much as he wanted her there.

He cuddled in behind her, like he'd done the last time she'd spent the night in his bed, his chin resting on the top of her head, his anterior in full contact with her posterior and his powerful arm draped over her ribs with his hand cupping her breast.

"Thank you," he said on a deep sigh.

No. Thank *you*. Jena closed her eyes and savored the feel of him. Just. For. Tonight. Her body relaxed, indulged in a closeness that would never be repeated.

Jena woke to darkness, her phone alarm going off. She lifted it to check the time—four o'clock—and stop the ringing. She listened for the twins, thrilled to hear nothing but quiet, thankful the noise hadn't set them off. So warm. She closed her eyes.

Someone moved behind her.

She sucked in a breath.

"What?" a male voice asked, pulling her close.

Justin. It all came back. His head wound. Stiches. A concussion. Hourly neurological checks. "What's your name?" she asked.

"Do you often wake up unsure who you're in bed with?" he mumbled, teasing her. Back to normal.

"You'd think with the wild, party-girl lifestyle I lead, I'd be used to it by now," she quipped.

He squeezed her. "Wise ass."

Only with him, probably because so many of their interactions over the years had occurred while she'd been pretending to be Jaci whose personality lent itself to sarcasm and playfulness. "I was checking to see your level of orientation or if I need to drag you back to the hospital."

"My name is Justin Rangore," he whispered.

"Now here's a toughie," she said, "Who am I?"

He rocked his hips. Something firm poked her butt cheek. "You are the lovely, and when I say lovely I mean alluring, sensual, and charming *Jena* Piermont."

His emphasis on "Jena" made her smile and delighted her beyond measure. She reset her alarm to go off in an hour. "Back to sleep," she said a bit surprised when he didn't balk and continue putting the moves on her and actually seemed to drift right back into slumber.

The next three times Jena's alarm startled her back to consciousness she could barely stay awake long enough to gently shake Justin, determine him to be oriented to person, place and time, and reset her alarm before falling back into an exhausted sleep.

"Hey, beautiful." A man's soft voice interrupted a delicious dream. Lips, she assumed his, pressed a kiss to the tip of her nose. "Rise and shine."

Lying on her side, Jena opened her eyes to sunshine and Justin's face less than an inch away. She slapped her hand over her mouth.

"Relax," he said so at ease with their position. "Two morning breaths cancel each other out."

"Are you speaking from your vast experience waking up in bed with women," she asked from behind her hand, "Or saying the first thing that came to mind to keep me from leaving the bed to gargle with mouthwash?"

"Yes." He smiled.

"How do you feel?" she asked.

He took the hand covering her mouth, slid it down his naked chest, to an impressive morning erection. "You tell me."

Oh my. Great. He felt great. Awesome. "Well, that's a pretty big indication you no longer need me around to take care of you." She started to roll away but came to an abrupt stop on her back, when Justin pounced on top of her, pinning her hips beneath his.

"But I do." He rested his upper body on his elbows and leaned down to kiss her cheek. "Don't go."

Somehow her knees parted and he settled in between them, his groin flush with hers, the pressure of his arousal…right there. She wanted to lift her hips. Needed…

He pushed some hair off of her forehead and stared deeply into her eyes. "Stay with me, Jena."

Jena. Stay with me, Jena. Not Jaci.

She shouldn't. Sex would only make her eventual choice of husband, and doing what was best for her and her daughters, more difficult. She glanced at the clock anyway. The girls would be up soon. Jena had never been separated from them for as long as they'd been apart over the last twenty-four hours. She ached to see their smiling faces and kiss their baby-scented skin. And it was too much to expect Jaci—

"Please," he said, the need in his voice, the rich, sensual timbre made her woman parts tingle. "I want to show you something." And Lord help her, Jena wanted to see it, feel it and experience it.

He rocked his hips. Slowly. Forward. Then back. The length of his erection providing an intimate massage that drove words like "stop" and "no" from cognition, leaving only synonyms of "yes", "more", and "faster" accessible for use.

"What?" On impulse she skimmed her hands down the soft skin covering his lateral ribs to his waist. "What do you want to show me?"

"How good I make love when I'm sober." He kept his voice quiet, seductive, as he lowered his mouth to her ear and whispered, "When I take my time, and my sole focus is your pleasure."

Jena couldn't contain a sensual shiver.

The little demonstration of "sole focus on her pleasure" that followed proved him a proficient and talented sexual multi-tasker.

Aroused Jena, the one listening to her stimulated, needy body crying out for one last sexual hurrah battled Rational Jena, the cautious, responsible one wedged in her head, over the pros and cons of crossing her ankles behind his butt, opening for him and exerting some control over the speed, depth and direction of his frustratingly languid pelvic activity.

Rational Jena won out. This time. But with each caress of her breast, each glide of his palm over her nipple, each slide of his erection along her swollen, moistening sex Aroused Jena was gaining strength.

"That's very altruistic of you," she teased. And very tempting. If she married Thomas goodbye sex life hello abstinence. Even if she held out in search of an understanding heterosexual male who could accept her treatment decisions—as if one would be easy to find within the next two months—from the research she'd done, after surgery she expected changes in the sensation, look and feel of her breasts that would impact both her and her partner in any future intimate relationship. This could be her last opportunity to enjoy the delicious tingle of aroused nipples, of a man's hands caressing her breasts and his mouth... "But don't you mean how good you are at sex?" Because making love would require, well...love. Or at least some degree of mutual affection.

He kissed the sensitive cove at the base of her ear. Oh so gentle. His hips maintained their unhurried rhythm. Forward. Then back. Over and over. His fingers teased. "How about I spend the next couple of hours demonstrating the difference?" He kissed along the line of her jaw to her chin. He touched his lips to hers. So tender, nothing like the mashing, passionate kisses she now associated with sex.

Sex. Not making love.

When he lifted his head she said, "We already had sex."

"Honey, I'm not proud to admit it, but what we had was a sloppy, drunken version of sex I want to eradicate from your memory." He started to slide down her body.

"Hey," she said. "I haven't agreed to anything." Yet.

He pushed up her cotton tee. "But you will." He set his mouth to her breast, swirled his tongue around her nipple, sucked and Oh. My. Goodness. Without conscious thought, "Yes," shot from her mouth like a cork from an agitated bottle of bubbly.

He moved to her other breast. The feel of his triumphant grin against her skin gave her pause. This is what Justin did. Seduce. Convince. Use whatever means necessary to get what he wanted. Being treated like just another conquest didn't sit right, regardless of how much she wanted him, so she forced out a, "Stop," and pushed him away.

He lifted his head and looked at her, confused. Surprised.

"Annie and Abbie will be up soon," she said. "I have to go."

She expected him to bargain or cajole.

He didn't.

He did, however, move up her body, slowly, setting his moist tongue to her neck for the last part of his journey up to whisper in her ear, "Tonight, then. After work." He blew out a hot, shaky breath. "Baby, tonight. What I'm going to do to you."

Jena swallowed, gulped actually, as an excited, adventurous, illicit anticipatory longing started to bubble deep within her.

"You look tired," Jena said, walking over to where Justin stood in the lobby of the urgent care center with his back resting up against the wall.

It was kind of sweet that she kept checking on him. "Because someone kept waking me up last night."

"Which is why tonight you need a good night's sleep," she tried, not for the first time, to get out of going back to his place.

She took him by the hand. "Justin is taking a quick

break, Gayle," she said then led him down the hall. "Come."

That was the plan. For both of them. Multiple times.

"I cannot believe you don't trust me enough to work without you watching over me like an overprotective parent," Jena complained. "You should be home in bed."

"Which is where I'd be right now if you'd agreed to stay there with me when I'd asked," he pointed out.

As she walked she chirped about headaches and blurred vision. Warning signs. Forgetfulness. Potential for delayed subdural hematoma. Permanent brain damage and dysfunction. Death.

While he chose to focus on his urge to release the thick curls restrained in her tight bun and muss them up for a wild, untamed look. But then they'd cover the smooth kissable, lickable skin at the back of her neck. His mouth actually watered at the thought. He moved his gaze lower, to the enticing sway of her hips and glimpses of the rounded perfectness of her butt each time her long top shifted.

Beyond her enticing physical attributes Justin found he actually enjoyed spending time with her which was a good thing since they'd spent so many hours in each other's presence over the past two days. Like the better part of his morning and early afternoon in Jena's bedroom, playing with the twins and learning to care for them. And while they slept, reviewing her financial statements, and teaching her to read them and pay her bills.

To date it'd been the longest period of time he'd ever spent in a room occupied by a bed and a woman without getting naked. And yet he'd still enjoyed himself, finding Jena a captivating mix of contrasts. Innocent yet sexy. Caring yet guarded. Insecure yet confident.

"Honestly," she said, jolting him back to the conversation. "I promised I wouldn't leave the building until Ian came to get me."

Like to protect her was the only reason he'd shown up at work. No, his motives way more self-serving, Justin had loaded up on acetaminophen so he could stay close to take advantage of every opportunity to entice her and remind her where they were headed at the end of her shift. To his bed where he would prove his attraction to *her* and not Jaci. Where he would make Jena crave him as much as he craved her. Where he would drive thoughts of Thomas and Dr. Charmer and a relationship with any other man right out of her head.

But she needed to get married. To someone. The mere thought of Jena tending to another man's wounds while dressed in her clingy pajamas, or cuddling up to another man in bed, caused his chest to tighten. As did thinking of binding himself to a woman, of disappointing her, and upsetting her over and over for five long years.

"I feel fine." Except for a residual nagging headache.

She pulled him into an empty exam room. "Sit." She pointed to a chair.

"Yes, ma'am." But only because he hoped maybe she'd come in close to check his stiches so he could— Yes! She walked toward the chair. He spread his knees in welcome and she moved between them.

Oh yeah.

He inhaled. "You smell so good." He set his hands at the backs of her knees, lightly. Testing. When she didn't react he moved up to the lusciously firm mounds of her butt. "Feel so good."

She ignored him. "Your incision line looks fine. Any headache?"

"No," he lied. Nothing would interfere with his plans for tonight.

"Blurred vision?"

He slid his hands up, under her scrub top to bare warm skin. "Nope."

She tried to step back.

He held her in place. "You didn't ask about my lips. They hurt." He looked up at her with what he hoped was a convincing sad expression. "I think a quick kiss would make them feel better."

She pushed on his shoulders, a half-hearted display if ever there was one. "Stop it." Her smile belied her tone of annoyance.

"After you kiss me." Obviously she needed more of an enticement so, holding her with one hand at her back, he moved his other hand around front, to her right breast, her nipple hard beneath his palm. "Breasts are my favorite part of the female anatomy. And yours are perfection." The nicest he'd seen, touched and tasted. No lie. Considering the number of women he'd been with over the years that was saying something. "I love that you don't wear a padded bra." So he could feel her arousal and revel in her response to his touch.

She let out a breath. "We can't."

He noticed she didn't make any attempt to flee.

Gotcha.

He moved his other hand around so he could caress both of her lovely breasts at the same time, lavishing attention on the rounded fullness of her perfect Cs,

watching the movement of her scrub top as he maneuvered underneath it, wishing he could see his hands on
her fair skin.

"My goodness you're making this hard."

"Well *you're* making *this* hard." He reached for her
hand and lowered it to his growing erection.

Major miscalculation.

She jerked her hand away like she'd received an electric shock. "This is so wrong." She glanced at the door
then at his crotch. "So unprofessional." She stepped
back. He let her go. "What if Mary came in with a patient?"

"She wouldn't open a closed door without knocking
first." But Jena was right. He'd gone too far. "Later."
He stared up at her. "Promise me."

She thought about it. "Okay," she agreed, backing
away from him. "Tonight." She turned to leave, mum-
bling something that sounded like, "One last time."

After the door closed Justin leaned back and shut
his eyes. Last time? Silly girl. They were just getting
started.

For the rest of their shift Jena didn't look him in
the eye. But she looked at other parts of him. And the
pink blush that erupted on her cheeks when he caught
her staring got him hotter than the most overt sexual
advances. "What's going on in that head of yours?"
he asked.

"Wouldn't you like to know?" She hurried off.

Why yes he would like to know, as a matter of fact.
What made one of the richest girls in town focus her
telescope on him? Choose him as her first lover? Trust
him to help her with her finances? Look at him with lust
in her eyes and treat him with caring when she could

have her pick of men? Better men, wealthy, cultured men more suited to circulating in her upper class circles.

A car screeched to a stop outside. Justin went on alert. A man jumped out of the driver seat, yanked on the rear passenger door, and pulled out a young child wearing blue pajamas. Justin held open the heavy glass door for him.

"My son," the man said, panting, his eyes wild. "He's having trouble breathing."

Justin looked down at the sleeping child cradled in the man's arms. Maybe two or three years old, his nose red, his eyes puffy, his lashes clumped with tears.

"Okay. Not right now," he said "But a few minutes ago he was crying and coughing, a strange barky cough that scared the hell out of me. He couldn't catch his breath. My wife is away on a business trip. I called the pediatrician who said it sounded like croup. What the hell is croup? And what kind of kook doctor diagnoses a child over the telephone?" The man shifted the boy so his head rested on his shoulder. "Drive to urgent care with the windows open, he told me."

"Seems to have worked," Justin commented, after filling in at the urgent care center dozens of times, very familiar with croup and this exact scenario.

Beyond listening, the man continued on as if Justin hadn't spoken. "If the coughing stops and Joshua calms down turn around and go back home, he told me. So the crying and coughing and gasping for breath can start up again in an hour? I don't think so. My son needs treatment. Right now. I want him examined by a doctor," the man demanded.

"That's why we're here," Justin replied. "Please sign in with Gayle." Justin directed the man to the registration desk. "I'll get a nurse to come out." Because he wasn't a medical professional and would rather Mary or Jena decide if the little boy needed to be taken right in.

He found Jena in the supply room carrying a pack of disposable diapers and a case of formula. "Where're these going?" He took them from her. "There's a little boy out front I'd like you to take a look at. Possible croup. The man with him is pretty upset."

"Exam room four," she said without argument. "Then they're ready to go."

An hour later, ten minutes to close, after a visit with a doctor and lots of instruction and reassurance from Jena, Justin accompanied Joshua and his dad out to the parking lot.

"Sorry about before," the man said.

"No need to apologize," Justin replied.

The man unlocked the car, opened the rear passenger door, and tucked Joshua into his car seat. When he emerged he asked, "You have kids?"

As of two days ago, "Yeah. Two little girls. Twins." He noticed he stood a bit taller, feeling rather proud about it.

"This parenthood gig is one crazy ride." The man shook his head.

Justin had no doubt it would be once he secured his spot on the parental rollercoaster beside Jena.

Who sure took her time cleaning up and restocking for the next day.

By half past twelve even Mary had had enough. "Come on, Jena," she called down the hallway. "I've got to get home. Max is waiting up for me." She turned to Justin. "With candles burning and lotion warming."

"Thanks for the visual but that's more information than I need to know."

"Tough. Do you think I want to go home and have sex? My son wakes up at sunrise. I won't get home until close to one in the morning. I need to sleep," Mary complained. "But I fear I inadvertently strayed into the path of those horny vibes pulsing back and forth between you and Jena. Heck, even Dr. Morloni set up a late night rendezvous. Did you see how fast he bolted out of here?"

Come to think of it, yes he had.

"Sorry. I'm ready," Jena said, walking toward them while slipping on her lavender sweater.

"Me, too," Mary said brightly.

"Me, three," Justin added, controlled, squelching a, "Halleluiah let's go home and get us laid", restraining the urge to grab Jena by the hand and make a mad dash to his SUV.

"Have fun, you two," Mary said with a sly smile and a wink as she slid into the front seat of her car.

"Oh, no," Jena said after Mary slammed her door shut. She grabbed his arm, pulling him to a stop and looking up, her expression lost in the darkness but concern evident in her tone. "Do you think she knows?"

"Knows what?" He played dumb, didn't want her distracted by unnecessary embarrassment.

"That we're going back to your place to… To…"

He found her prim inability to speak the words for what they were headed to do, amusing. Refreshing. So different from his usual women. "Get naked? Have sex? Renew our intimate acquaintance? Get it on? Make love?" he teased.

She smacked his chest. "I'm serious."

"Me, too." He tucked her hand in the crook of his

arm and headed to his SUV. "This parking lot at night is not a place to hang around talking." No matter how entertaining he found the topic of conversation.

Subject effectively changed, he slid his free hand into his pants pocket to grip the tactical folding knife he'd placed there before work. Only a fool with a death wish would try to jump him tonight.

On the walk into the condo complex Jena admitted, "I'm a little nervous."

Justin stopped.

"Now that you're sober," she said not looking at him. "And you know I'm not Jaci, what if you find me...lacking? Disappointing? What if you can't...?"

"Whoa!" He held up both hands. "Stop with the crazy talk." Justin Rangore had never as in N*E*V*E*R*E*V*E*R* been unable to get it up for a woman.

But this wasn't only about him. He hadn't missed the genuine concern in Jena's voice. Thankful for the benefit of standing under a large outdoor lighting fixture, he looked down into the beautiful blue eyes looking up at him, worried, vulnerable, searching for reassurance.

And he gave it to her. "Honey." He took her cold hands in his. "I have been craving you since this morning, fantasizing about you, counting the minutes until I could be with you. There is no way you could disappoint me."

"Sometimes," she turned her head away. "When we want something so much we dream about it and yearn for it and fantasize what it'll be like, we set unrealistically high expectations for how amazing it'll be. And when it isn't, the disappointment is so much worse than never having it at all."

Pow! A verbal uppercut to the diaphragm. Quite painful, actually. *He'd* disappointed *her*, had been in too much of a rush. An experienced woman knew how to find her pleasure. Had the confidence to ask for it and convey her likes and wants. An inexperienced woman needed to be shown her options, taught the possibilities, and encouraged to vocalize her desires.

The teacherly aspect turned out to be a pretty big turn on, as was her honesty and trusting him enough to share her concern. It made him determined to do better. To prove his attraction to *her*. To give her the spectacular night of loving she deserved. A night to remember. Always. No matter what happened in the morning.

He pulled her close, lifted her chin, and set his lips to hers. "Neither one of us will be disappointed tonight." He kissed her again. "I promise."

He stepped back and held out his hand, palm up in invitation. And waited.

With a small smile she placed her hand in his. Trusting him. Believing in him. No gesture ever meant more.

In the lobby Brandon, the concierge, waved and called out, "Hi, Jaci. Hi, Justin."

Without hesitation Jena smiled and waved. "Hi, Brandon. How's your mom feeling?"

"Much better," he said. "Thanks for asking."

Justin saw the man every day and had never once discussed his mother. He doubted Jaci had either. "Why didn't you correct him?"

Jena pushed the up arrow at the elevators and shrugged. "It's easier not to. I'm the shy twin. The quiet twin. The smart and obedient twin. Jaci's fun and friendly and popular. I don't mind people thinking I'm her." She glanced up with sad eyes. "Usually."

Then she looked down at her feet. "Anyway, I'm tired of always being the good twin."

In the elevator Justin said, "I bet if you'd give people the chance to get to know you they'd find you're friendly and they'd like you, too." He pushed her up against the metallic coated wall. "Take me for instance." He bent to tongue her ear. "I like you."

She trembled.

"I like you, too," she said quietly.

He picked her up at the back of her thighs, wrapping her legs around his hips so he could rub his hardon between her legs, to show her how much he liked her. "And if you're looking to let your bad girl out for a little play time, you have come to the right place."

He rocked his hips.

She let out a breath and dropped her forehead to his shoulder. "Lord help me, being bad feels so good."

"Baby you ain't seen nothing yet."

CHAPTER SIX

WITH a ping the elevator doors opened. And rather than put her down, Justin took a step. Like he planned to exit with her wrapped around him like a tree-hugging coconut-picker. With a total disregard for who might see them. "Put me down." She tried to wiggle free, wasted energy when a man as strong as Justin wasn't on board with the put-me-down plan. "Seriously," she said. "My burgeoning bad girl isn't ready for public displays." And probably never would be.

He loosened his arms just enough for her to shimmy down over that very prominent, very hard, very male, very dream-worthy part of him. "Behind-closed-doors-bad-girl works for me, too," he said with a wink. Then he walked out of the elevator, looked back over his shoulder, and flashed her a cocky but oh-so-sexy follow-me-for-a-good-time smile. So handsome and confident.

And follow him she did, but not before the elevator doors started to close. Shoot. She darted in between them and, not wanting to come off overly eager or desperate to feel his hands on her, even though she was, she walked at a moderate pace until she reached his side. He set his heavy arm across her shoulders and pulled her close.

An act of possession? Protection? Preventing escape?

It didn't matter. She liked it.

Inside his condo, without even taking the time to turn on the lights, he slammed the door closed and gave her More—with a capital M. Again he lifted her feet from the floor. Again he pressed her back to the wall and positioned his hips between her wide open thighs, pressing and rubbing where she wanted pressing and rubbing the most. Only he added a wet, aggressive, breath-stealing, tongue-probing, passion-inducing kiss that had her twisting her fingers in his hair, pulling his mouth even closer, and grinding against him like some uninhibited, lust-crazed, sex fiend.

Apparently her inner bad girl didn't require much coaxing to come out in Justin's presence.

He pulled back, breathing heavy. "My, God, Jena. You feel so good. I'm having a hard time controlling myself."

My, God, Jena. You feel so good. Jena. Not Jaci. Justin admitted having a hard time controlling himself because of Jena. The only thing that could have improved that moment was if she'd had the wherewithal to record his statement for future listening pleasure.

He rested his forehead on hers. "If we don't slow it down I'm going to take you right here, right now. Just. Like. This." He punctuated each of his final three words with a delicious thrust of his hips. More promise than threat.

She wanted to yell, "Do it! Let passion take over. Give in to your urgent need to take me hard and fast like you'll die if you don't." Like she'd seen time after time in the romantic movies she watched in the quiet loneliness of her bedroom, wishing to be the recipient of rip-your-clothes-off, got-to-have-you-now, can't-wait-

the-time-it'd-take-to-get-to-the-bedroom desire at least
once in her life. And since this particular moment in
time might turn out to be her last chance to experience
it, Jena quietly said, "That'd be okay."

He let out a breath. "I am barely holding it together,
Jena. Don't tease."

"I'm not." She needed him. So bad. Tonight. Now.

He leaned down to her ear and whispered, "Tell me
what you want."

"This."

He chuckled. "In detail. I want to make tonight special for you. Tell me what you want." He blew out a puff
of hot air and tongued the inner rim of her ear, setting
off waves of lust throughout her body. At the same time
he set his hand on her breast, teasing her nipple into a
tight, aroused peak. Between her legs, the entrance to
her body throbbed with its yearning to be filled by him.

"Please," she begged.

"Please, what?" he asked seductively, his lips tickling
her ear as he spoke, his hand moving to her other breast.

"Please, don't make me ask. You know what I want.
What I need." Normally, Jena would have left it at that
and whatever happened, happened. However, seemed
her bad girl wasn't taking any chances and Jena found
herself turning toward his ear, and, with the same hot
puff of breath he gave her, demanding, in the most de-
mure voice she could muster, "Now strip me naked and
give it to me." As if someone else had taken control of
her body her hips rocked along his erection in three
long slow strokes. "Just. Like. This."

Through the thin fabric of her scrub pants and lace
panties his hard heat warmed and aroused her. Bring
her higher. Making her ache. "I need—"

"I know what you need, honey."

Evidently somewhere between direction and perception some pertinent information got lost because he lowered her to a standing position which was not at all what she needed. Yet her words of protest got sucked down her throat on a gasp of surprise when he tugged off her sweater, lifted her scrub top in one smooth motion, and unhooked her bra with ease before pulling it off and flinging it aside. Then he matched her half-naked by yanking his shirt off.

That's more like it. She lunged forward and wrapped her arms around him. Bare breasts to naked chest, loving the feel of him, focusing in on every detail, every sensation, making a memory that would have to last a lifetime.

"I'm liking your bad girl," he said, his hands at work untying her drawstring.

"Me, too." She kissed his shoulder, licked and sucked his skin into her mouth. "Seems she only comes out for you."

"Good." Her pants slid to the floor. "Let's keep it that way." Justin followed them down, taking her panties with him. Seconds later she stood naked, except for a pair of socks, darkness the only thing keeping her from total mortification. Her body had changed since their last time together, and not for the better.

Justin stood.

Yes.

The light in the entryway came on.

No.

"Turn it off," she cried, hunching forward, trying to cover her abdomen with her hands. She didn't want him to see...

"I don't want us to be two anonymous people making out in the dark. I want to see you. Watch you—"

No. "Turn it off," she yelled, trying to swivel away from him. She wanted the dark, the covert encounter, even though her current blemishes were nothing compared to the metamorphosis to come.

"Hey." He took her by the shoulders and held her in place. Gentle but firm. "What's wrong?" He lowered his gaze to her hands.

Don't. "I have to go." She never should have come, would never measure up to the women Justin favored. Slim. Beautiful. Perfect.

"Talk to me," he said. So calm. Concerned.

"Only if you turn off the light."

He looked at her like she was an absolute crazy person, justifiably so. But finally did.

Only she no longer took comfort in the darkness because now she wanted to leave and couldn't see her clothes.

"The light is off," he pointed out. "And it occurs to me you gave birth to two babies six weeks ago and I don't know if you had surgery or delivered them via the regular route. Or if you're all healed and we should even be doing this."

"If I wasn't healed, I wouldn't be here," she said.

He stood quietly, offering no response.

"I'm naked and I'm cold and would rather have this conversation with some clothes on." Or not at all worked.

"Not a chance." He picked her up, his body warming hers on contact. When she didn't immediately wrap her legs around his waist—which took quite a bit of restraint, mind you—he took one leg and then the other and did it for her. Then, in the limited light from a cloudy night, he carried her to the couch.

"The doctor told you no heavy lifting." Which had completely slipped her mind the two times he'd hoisted her up against a wall and held her there. Bad nurse.

"Nice try."

He sat down with her facing him, her thighs spread across his lap, pulled her chest to his, and covered them both with a knit blanket. "Now talk."

"I delivered both girls vaginally and my doctor told me I could resume sexual activity at six weeks."

"Good." He thrust his hips up.

"I *could*," she emphasized. "Not I *should* or I *had to*. And upon further consideration I've decided to wait." She tried to slide off of him. No chance of that happening. But in her wide open state, with him still impressively firm, her attempts provided some much welcome stimulation which ramped up her heretofore waning arousal. Yum! She started to rock in earnest. "My goodness, I like this position."

"Me, too." He pushed down on her butt while he moved beneath her, skilled at massaging the exact right spot. "Just think. All I have to do is unzip my pants, slip on a condom and I could be inside you. Ten seconds tops."

Worked for her. End of conversation about her body. A night of fabulous sex with Justin sober and at the top of his game. A night to indulge and be thankful for this last randy rendezvous with all her parts present and in full working order. She fought the urge to shave off precious seconds by telling him to forget the condom she was on birth control—because never again would she leave her protection to someone else. But the con-

dom was the right choice for reasons other than preventing pregnancy and even with her good sense hazy
with lust, she knew that. "Do it." She reached between
them to help.

He clasped her hands in his. "After you explain your
vampire-like exposed to sunlight routine when I turned
on the light."

Party pooper. "Here I was just starting to enjoy myself again." And she could tell he was, too. So, taking
advantage of his arousal, she rubbed her breasts from
side to side across his chest making sure to shift her
body over his erection at the same time. "Sex now. Talk
later." Much. And if he happened to fall asleep before
the talking, and she happened to slip away in the dead
of night to go take care of her babies? Oh well.

"Talk now." He stayed her hips "Sex every hour on
the hour until we're too exhausted to move, later."

A tempting offer. A wonderful, stupendous, amazingly excellent offer. Except for the talk now. "You're
so eager to know? You can't wait until morning? You
want to ruin absolutely everything?"

He didn't respond. Didn't move.

She sat up. "Fine. My body. It's not the same as the
last time we were together."

He sat in silence. Waiting. Darn stubborn man.

She let out a breath. Might as well get it over with
so she could get home and get some sleep before the
twins woke up. "I've got stretch marks, okay? Ugly red
stretch marks from the pregnancy. They're a total turn
off and I had hoped to get through this night without
you seeing them." She pushed off his chest and started
to climb off his lap. "You happy now?"

"Wait." He palmed her hips and held her in place.

"I decide what turns me on and what turns me off. Not you."

"Trust me, you like pretty and they are not pretty. Now let me go."

He shifted on the couch, leaned to the side, and holy cow—turned on a lamp.

"Are you kidding me?" She wrapped the blanket fully around her. "Is today opposite day? I say one thing you do another? Rather juvenile if you ask me. As is not taking another person's feelings into account and being plain old mean."

He looked up at her. Serious. Thoughtful. "I think you giving birth to my daughters is a beautiful thing. I think you are a beautiful woman. And a few marks on your skin aren't going to change my mind."

Gonad-guided guy focused on external beauty and women as a recreational activity that he was, she doubted that.

He reached for the edges of the blanket she had clutched tightly in her fists. "Please," he said in such a way she relaxed her hold and allowed him to open the sides of the blanket, giving him a full view of her torso.

To Jena's surprise he showed no immediate reaction as he studied her. She knew what he saw, loose skin around her navel and numerous dark pink squiggly lines at the base of her belly spreading out toward her hips. "They look tender," he said. "Do they hurt?"

"Only my body image," she replied and for some reason felt the need to explain. "The nurse at the doctor's office said they'll fade in time. But I fear my bikini days are over."

He ran a finger down a particularly large, offensive

looking one. "You've been through so much, changes to your body and your life, because of me."

Okay. That was not at all the reaction she'd expected. She studied him back, the strange look on his face. Far from the revulsion she'd expected. More wonder, mixed with concern and was she totally out of her mind to think maybe a bit of caring?

"I wouldn't change a thing," Jena said. Meaning it. "I love the girls. I love being a mother." And she was kind of looking forward to being a wife, cooking for her man, whoever he turned out to be, managing their home and their lives, planning her daughters' futures.

"I still think you're beautiful, Jena," he said, looking up at her, sounding so sincere.

Lying rather convincingly. "Keep talking that blarney and I won't be able to trust anything that comes out of your mouth."

"Okay. You're right," he said with a dramatic sigh. "They're hideous. I can't stand to look at them." He shielded his eyes.

"Hey." She slapped his shoulder. "That's not nice."

He let out an exaggerated huff of frustration. "I can't win. I tell you you're beautiful, you say I'm full of blarney—a word I haven't heard used in casual conversation since Timmy Oswald and I played pirate back in elementary school, by the way. I tell you you're hideous and you tell me I'm not nice. And physically assault me."

"I did not—"

"Is there any pleasing you?" He slid both hands up to her breasts and squeezed her nipples between the V of two fingers while staring down at her sex. He licked his lips and said, "I think I know a way."

The blood drained from Jena's upper body, pooling in hot, pulsing need between her legs. "I hope it involves you finally removing your pants."

He smiled. "Among other things."

Her teenage fantasy about to play out in real heart-pounding, breath-gasping, pleasure-finding life. Starring Jena and Justin as themselves.

"But first," he said. "Kiss me, Jena. Then I'm all yours. Tell me what you want. Show me. Ask me. Anything."

Anything...

I still think you're beautiful, Jena. Kiss me, Jena. Justin made it a point to use her name often and planned to keep repeating it. So there'd be no question. No doubt. So she'd know for certain his every word was intended for her alone.

Jena pressed her lips to his in what turned out to be so much more than the lusty, desirous prelude to sex he'd expected. Starting off slow, with gentle touches moving along his lip line, she cupped his cheeks between her soft palms, before taking the kiss deeper. And not in a physical way. But with a fervor he hadn't expected. Unrestrained affection. A bonding. A sealing of fates and futures.

Yet rather than putting a stop to the surge of intense feelings flowing at him to give her the 'Don't make this out to be more than it is' speech, Justin hugged her close and kissed her back, upping the ferocity. Taking what she offered and giving her more in return. For the first time allowing himself to feel an emotional connection. To the girl who'd watched him from her mansion up on the hill. The woman who'd chosen him as her first and only lover. The mother of his children.

When they finally broke for air Jena said, "I don't want sex."

Disappointment threatened to suffocate him.

"I want you to make love to me."

Can do.

She slowed them down with another soul-searing, yearning-filled, delicately passionate kiss. "Like you would to a woman you really care about. Someone who matters."

Wait a minute. He went rigid. She mattered.

"If you can't… I mean don't want to—" She misunderstood.

"No. It's just—"

"Don't ruin the mood." She kissed him. "It's okay." She moved her fingers to the button of his pants and he let her. While he came to terms with the fact he did care about her. For so many reasons. Like their clandestine encounters in high school. The cakes she made for him. The way she cared for Jaci, his daughters, her patients, and him after he'd been injured.

That he cared for her, too, was the only explanation for the level of fear he'd felt at the thought of her alone in that parking lot, not knowing what those thugs planned to do, doing to her, and the degree of anger he'd experienced when he'd seen a man slip his arm around her neck in a chokehold. Both disturbing, and so much more powerful than a police officer typically felt for a victim or random acquaintance in a similar situation. And then there was the painful ache that'd tightened his insides at the thought of him and his girls having to live life without her…

"You okay?" she asked.

"Yeah." Considering in the course of the last forty-eight hours his past as he knew it, his present as he lived it, and his future as he'd envisioned it, had all been altered by the woman in his arms.

"Then how about a little help here?" She tugged at the waistband of his pants. "If there's a way to get these off while I'm sitting on your lap I haven't been able to figure it out. The way I see it, either you need to clue me in to the disrobing secret or let go of me so I can move around a little."

That's when he realized he had his arms clamped around her in a bear hug someone three times her size wouldn't have been able to escape. "Sorry." He released her.

"Now that's more like it." In a move sexier than the most seasoned seductress had in her arsenal of allure, Jena slid off his lap, taking his pants and briefs with her. He lifted his butt, grabbing his wallet out of his back pocket and placing it on the arm of the sofa.

She came to a stop, kneeling on the floor at his feet, her lovely, naked body between his now bare thighs. In the light of the lamp she looked him over. "*You're* the one who's beautiful," she said.

At his erection her eyes went wide. Then her tongue made an appearance, glossing her lips and Justin almost lost it. "Not that I wouldn't love for you to do what you're thinking." He reached for his wallet. "But tonight is for you." Mostly.

She smiled. "I like the sound of that."

"Baby, you're going to like what comes next even better." He took out a condom and held it up. "How about we do this together to make sure it's in good working order?"

She nodded.

He ripped open the wrapper and handed her the ring of latex.

She took it while admitting, "I've never done this before."

He liked being the one to share her firsts. He also liked the eager interest in her eyes as she stared at his proud member, standing full and tall. For her.

"Like this." He took her hands and set the condom on the tip. Together they rolled it on. No visible rips or deformities. "Looks good."

"Yessiree, it does," she said. "Now can we *finally* get to the good stuff?"

Oh yeah. He leaned forward and lifted her high enough to get an eyeful of magnificent breasts. "Straddle me." She did, resting her knees on the sofa beside his hips. He shifted them and, using both hands on her bottom, spread her wide and directed her down until the head of his erection slid ever-so-slightly into the slick heat of her opening. Teasing. Tempting. Torturing.

She moaned. "That feels so good."

Yes. It. Did. He said a quick prayer to the God of endurance. "This is only the beginning." He leaned forward and gave her lovely nipples some attention while taking quick, shallow dips inside of her.

"More," she said, her hands gripping the sides of his head below his stiches, holding him close.

He lowered her while pushing up into her moist heat. *Stay in control*. Up then out. *So damn good*. Advancing a bit further each time. *Keep it slow*. Deeper. *Atta girl, take it all*. Until fully surrounded. *Amazing*. "My,

God, you feel good, Jena." He fought the powerful urge
to pound into her, hard and fast, to bring them both to
climax. No more talking. No more waiting. Satisfaction. Now.

But that's not what she wanted. At least it's not what
she'd asked for. *"...make love to me. Like you would to
a woman you really care about. Someone who matters."*
And to do that he'd need to stay in control.

"Hang on," Justin said, wrapping her arms around
his shoulders. And with them still joined together he
pushed up off the couch and cradled her butt in his
hands. "I've got you."

"Now what?" she asked.

He started to walk.

"Oh." She wiggled her bottom. "I like this, too."

And suddenly five years of marriage—to Jena—
didn't seem all that daunting. Hell, neither did ten or
twenty. Balancing her on one hand, he flicked on the
lamp by the bed.

"You scared of the dark?" she asked. Teasing. "Your
electric bill must be astronomical."

"Ha. Ha." He lowered them to the bed. "Next time
we'll do it by candlelight, flashlight, or sans light. Your
call. But for right now I can't wait one more minute." He
set her on her back, went up on his elbows and looked
into her eyes. "To watch you come. Keep your feet
crossed behind my back." He pulled out and sank deep.

She inhaled and arched her spine as her eyes rolled
back in her head.

"You like that." He did it again.

She nodded. "A lot."

"Good." He lowered his mouth to hers and kissed her
deeply. Pressure began to build. *Too soon.* He swiveled

his hips. She moaned. *Good.* He fondled her nipple. She turned her head and groaned. *Better.* "Tell me what you want," he said.

"This," she answered rocking to meet his thrusts. "You."

"I want you, too, Jena." And not just for tonight. "Only you."

Her eyes shot open.

He stared into them. "You matter," he said. "To me." She tightened her inner muscles and squeezed him so tight he lost focus. And it was his turn to close his eyes and take the pleasure she offered. No. Jena first.

He forced his eyes open to find her smiling. "Kegel exercises."

"I'm a fan." He scooted up, made sure each long, deep thrust slid along the epicenter of her arousal, effectively wiping the smile from face, and increased his pace. "You're beautiful, Jena…smart…sexy." He took a moment to try to catch his breath. "We're so good together." In sync. "I—"

"Justin," she cried out.

"Come for me." He reveled in her panting and high-pitched moans.

"Hold me," she cried, reaching for him.

He dropped down, hugging, kissing, and loving her, finding his satisfaction mere seconds after she did. Then he rolled onto his side, taking her with him, to ride out a sweet new life-changing contented bliss in her arms.

The next morning Justin woke to a warm, naked Jena curled up against his side, her head on his upper arm, her leg slung over his thigh. He smiled. A cuddler. And for once he didn't mind. Didn't think about how he could slip away without waking his lover or what excuse he'd use to get rid of her. Quite the opposite, he spent some time enjoying the feel of her, thinking that making it a regular thing, a permanent thing, wouldn't be so bad.

He waited for the dread that typically accompanied thoughts of being stuck with one woman on a long term basis, the resentment and defiance that typically accompanied him feeling forced to do something he didn't want to do, and felt only a happy contentment with the idea of marriage to Jena, with sleeping beside her night after night, living with her and taking care of her and their daughters, his family.

Now all he had to do was convince Jena to marry him.

He glanced at the clock, knowing, good mother that she was, Jena would want to get home before the girls woke up. That gave him about twenty minutes, fifteen to work off his morning arousal and five to bring up the topic of marriage while she was suspended in the afterglow of orgasm.

Carefully, he turned to face her, easing his thigh deeper between her legs, palming her butt, pulling her close which set his growing erection against her belly. He caressed her leg and hip up her side to cup her breast.

She stretched.

"Morning, beautiful," he whispered.

With her eyes still closed she gave him a sleepy smile and rotated her pelvis. "Three times wasn't enough?"

The bed. The shower. The kitchen table after their three a.m. refueling.

"I'm afraid not." It didn't feel like he'd ever get his fill of her. "What do you say?" He turned to his back pulling her on top of him. "We haven't done it like this yet." And she'd sure liked being on top on the couch.

She pushed up on her arms to look at the clock then reached into the bedside drawer where he kept his condoms. Pulling one out she smiled and said, "I think I'd like to try out a quickie."

Compatibility in the bedroom.

They were off to a good start.

Within seconds she had him sheathed and lined up and was sinking down on top of him. "Lean forward and open your legs wider. Up and down." He guided her hips. "Take a little at a time. That's it."

How could she still be so tight after last night? And having twins?

Jena set her hands on his chest and took him deep. "I like this."

He liked her honesty, among other things. "Me, too." He gave up the battle to lie quietly and let her take her pleasure. "Now get moving." He arched his back and drove into her. "Quickie means quick."

She rode him hard and fast, rocking, repositioning, experimenting.

Justin shifted beneath her varying the depth and direction of his thrusts until—

"Oh," she cried out her eyes wide.

Found it.

Holding her steady to maintain their exact position he directed her to, "Lean back and put your hands on my knees."

She did. And he massaged her G-spot over and over. "My goodness," she said. "That's…"

Yes indeed. He didn't slow down until Jena cried out, flooding him with her pleasure. Justin bent up his knees to keep her from falling, giving him just enough time to grab her arms and pull her forward, where he held her tightly to his chest as he found his own release.

After a few minutes Jena stirred. "That was…" she started.

Indescribably amazing. "Yeah."

"So much better than I'd ever thought possible," she finished.

Providing him with the perfect segue. "I agree." He twirled a finger in one of her unruly curls. "Us together is so much better than I ever thought possible." He hugged her. "You're funny and sweet and caring and beautiful and sexy. And while I doubt I'm the type of guy you ever pictured yourself marrying, I will try my hardest to be a good husband to you and father to our girls. So what do you say? Will you marry me?"

She didn't respond.

"I'll get a ring. A nice one," he said. She just laid there. Limp. Heck, she didn't even seem to be breathing. "Hey." He shook her shoulders. Far from the excited "yes" he'd hoped for, she'd gone catatonic.

"Is this about my stupid 'five years isn't so long' comment? Because that came out all wrong."

Nothing.

Making love to her, making her feel special and cared for hadn't been enough. Justin felt his recently reconfigured plans for the future slipping out of reach. In a last ditch attempt to convince her he broke into a desperate babble. "I know there are no guarantees but we like each other." He looked down at the top of her head. "At least I like you. And I think you like me. And we both want what's best for our daughters. And we're good in the sack so that's a start, right?"

She lifted her head and looked at him with dead eyes. "What if I wasn't beautiful and sexy. And what if we weren't good in the sack? Would you still want to marry me?"

And they were back to that. Damn women and their ability to twist around everything a guy said. He answered one way he was a liar, another way he'd prove her point.

"I didn't think so," she said, pushing off of him and with an evil squint of her eyes, daring him to try and stop her.

"Give a guy a chance to speak, will you?"

She stopped at the side of the bed. Just sat there staring in the direction of his bedroom door, giving him a view of her back.

"You keep asking me questions I don't have the answers to," Justin said, angling his pillows against the headboard. This was a conversation he needed to sit up for. "Do you want me to lie to make you happy? Should I say I will always find you pretty? That I will always love your body no matter what? That from today until the day I die I will never ever find another woman as sexy you?"

She dropped her head to look down at her lap but didn't say a word.

"I can't predict the future, Jena. All I can do is be completely honest in telling you I want to marry you. And I give you my solemn vow to try my hardest, to respect you and take care of you and the girls for at least five years so you meet the terms of your trust."

She stiffened.

He rushed to add, "Does that mean I'm planning to run out and start divorce proceedings the second your fifth check clears? No. Does it mean we're going to live out our entire lives in wedded bliss? I hope so, but I just don't know. What newly married couple does?"

"Did you know my mother died of cancer?" Jena asked.

Finally she spoke. Totally off topic but he'd run with it. "No. I thought she died from pneumonia."

"Secondary to metastatic lung cancer that spread from her breast. I'd been so busy providing her day to day care after the traumatic brain injury, I had no idea the cancer had returned."

Justin had a vague recollection of Jaci mentioning her mother's breast cancer in passing maybe back in seventh or eighth grade.

"From the time of her first diagnosis mom and dad's relationship changed. Cancer wasn't pretty. Cancer showed weakness. Imperfection. Mom tried to maintain life as we knew it but dad started spending more and more time at the office. Chemotherapy made her sick, surgery made her sore and radiation therapy made her too tired to do much of anything."

Justin listened but had no idea where she was headed or what her mother had to do with them getting married.

"At the age of thirteen I took over managing the house and the staff and taking care of mom."

While Jaci spent hours after school and on weekends hanging out with him and their friends.

"When her beautiful blond hair started falling out clump by clump I helped her find ways to hide it. I accompanied her to treatments and held the basin while she vomited and retched. I saw my father, who'd once loved her dearly, look at her with distaste and regret. I watched helplessly as my vibrant, loving mom retreated inside of herself, trying to hide from the sickness and fear, growing more and more depressed as her life spiraled out of control. I gave up my teens to take care of her, and while I wouldn't have had it any other way, I refuse to put my daughters in the same position."

Wait a minute. Justin moved to sit beside her on the bed. "Are you trying to tell me you have breast cancer like your mother?" At the age of twenty-four? Were they doomed to months instead of years? Would he have to raise their daughters without her?

CHAPTER SEVEN

"No. Goodness, no," Jena said, feeling very naked and self-conscious with him sitting next to her.

"Thank God." He sounded relieved.

Unfortunately the story didn't end there. "But I tested positive for the BRCA2, commonly referred to as the breast cancer gene, mutation, which means I have an increased lifetime risk of developing breast and/or ovarian cancer accompanied by an increased risk of developing those cancers at an early age." Before menopause.

She stood and walked toward the door, trying not to think about him watching her naked butt jiggle.

"Hey. We're in the middle of a conversation here. Where are you going?"

"To get my clothes." She came to her turquoise lace bra hanging off the back of a black leather recliner chair first and slipped it on.

"I'm trying real hard to understand, but I think I'm going to need some clarification, small male brain and all." Justin strolled into the living room wearing a pair of navy boxer briefs and nothing else, his body absolute perfection, a total distraction. "What exactly does your mom having cancer and you taking care of her have to do with us getting married?"

Did he honestly miss the part about her having a significantly increased risk of developing the disease, too? Jena pulled up her matching lace panties, stepped into last night's scrub pants and glanced at the clock on the microwave in Justin's kitchen. "I have time for the short version." She tied the string at her waist.

Justin sat down on the couch, leaned back calm as can be and crossed his ankle over his knee. "Go."

Jena picked up her scrub top.

"You know I think I'd enjoy what you're about to tell me a lot more if you kept that off." He smiled.

She pulled it over her head. "I found the first painful lump in my breast at age twenty."

His smile vanished.

"Since that first lump I've found two more for a total of three in four years. The most recent five months ago."

"Jena." He sat up, Mr. Relaxation transformed into Mr. Concern. "I had no idea."

She cocked her head. "You know this will go a lot quicker if you save all comments and questions to the end." Please just let her say what had to be said without making her discuss every detail.

"Sorry," he said, leaning back. "Go on."

"That's three painful lumps, three rounds of repeat diagnostic testing, and three needle biopsies, the second one followed by a small lumpectomy, which were all negative, thank goodness." She bent over to slip on a sock.

"But each time, from finding the lump until I got back the final laboratory report, I spent day and night in a state of panic. What if it's cancer? What stage is it? What are my treatment options? My prognosis? My life expectancy?" She slipped on the other sock. "This last time was particularly rough." Being pregnant with twins, away from home, and unable to visit her regular doctors.

"I can't even imagine," he said quietly, more to himself than her, so she let it slide.

"I'm a mother now. A single mother responsible for two babies. What happens to them if I get sick and can't care for them? What happens if I die?" And per usual, whenever she thought of her daughters growing up without her, Jena's chest burned with sadness and a lump of despair balled in her throat.

"I—" Justin started.

"No." Jena held up a finger and cut him off. Because for the purposes of her decision making, the issue was not who would care for the twins, only that if she did not take action to decrease her risk of developing cancer, it might not be her wiping their tears, kissing them goodnight, or cuddling with them before bed. It most likely would not be her talking to them about boys or shopping for their prom dresses or planning their weddings. And no matter how loving her replacement might be, the overwhelmingly distressing fact that it would be someone other than Jena left her heartbroken.

"I can't live with the threat of cancer looming," she went on. "Feeling like I'm on death row, my days on earth numbered, not worrying about *if* it will strike but *when*. I need to take control of my life. For me. For my daughters." She slipped her feet into her clogs, walked to the recliner, and sat down facing Justin. "I've researched my situation and learned about genetic testing. I spent hours with a geneticist—which is largely responsible for maxing out my credit cards—discussing the risks and possible outcomes of testing, addressing why I wanted the test, what I planned to do with the information, and convincing her I wouldn't allow a positive result to negatively affect my life and my relationships."

"Yet you *are* letting it negatively affect *our* relationship," Justin pointed out.

Maybe, but to protect them both. "Well we didn't have a relationship at the time. And it's not affecting our relationship in the way you think." How to explain... "People handle the results of their genetic testing differently. I've decided to take a proactive approach. I have two first degree relatives—my mother and her sister—who were both diagnosed with breast cancer before menopause. My aunt found her first lump around age twenty-five. Stage three. She died before her thirtieth birthday."

Justin looked stunned.

Try sharing genetics with a woman first diagnosed at the age Jena would be turning in two and a half months.

"My mom didn't make it to fifty, granted she had other contributing factors. As for me, at a young age I've been diagnosed with dense breasts, another risk factor for developing breast cancer, and I've tested positive for a harmful genetic mutation. Yet instead of feeling doomed, I feel empowered."

His mouth opened but nothing came out.

So she kept the conversation going. "Because based on my research and evaluation of my cancer risk and the results of my genetic testing I can make a rational, educated, informed decision on how I want to proceed. *Before* cancer invades my life. I'm in control." Jena took a deep fortifying breath in preparation for the next part. "Which is why I've decided to undergo bilateral prophylactic mastectomies with immediate reconstruction and, at some date in the future, after I decide for certain

I don't want any more children, but no later than age thirty-five, a total abdominal hysterectomy."

Justin stared at her blankly. Information overload. Understandable. Been there.

"Prophylactic?" he asked.

"As in preventative or protective. Removing the breast tissue will significantly *reduce* my risk of developing breast cancer."

"Does it eliminate the risk?"

"No." She shook her head. "Because it's impossible to remove all the breast tissue."

"So." He stood. "Just so I'm sure I understand." He crossed one arm over his waist, rested the elbow of the other on his wrist, and traced his goatee in a downward motion with his index finger and thumb. "You're planning to have two major elective—am I correct in assuming they're elective?" He looked down at her for confirmation.

She nodded

"Two major *elective* surgeries that will disfigure your body and put you at risk for any number of surgical complications, because there's a chance that you *may*, at some point in the future, develop cancer." He moved both hands to his hips. "And you honestly think *you're* in control not the threat of cancer?"

"I can do without your sarcasm, thank you very much." Jena stood, too. "I knew you wouldn't understand and that you'd completely miss the point and focus in on the breast surgery and nothing else. Because heaven forbid the woman you marry didn't have big, beautiful, *real* breasts. They're your favorite part of the female anatomy, after all. And that, in a nutshell, is why no, I won't marry you. Bottom line, it's my body, and I decide how I will take care of it. You," she pointed, "don't get a say."

She turned to leave but stopped short to look over her shoulder and add, "And for the record, deciding to have surgery to significantly decrease my high risk of developing cancer gives me a control I wouldn't have once the cancer cells invade my body. No chemotherapy. No radiation therapy. No living with the threat of dying," she ticked each one off on her index, middle then ring finger, "day after day for months while waiting to see if the treatments were effective. You don't know what it's like." Tears leaked out of her eyes and ran down her cheeks as she remembered her mother's torturous battle against the disease. "As long as I have the choice, I choose life. And if choosing life means I have to live it without a pair of breasts and a uterus, then so be it." Jena continued on to the door, had to leave or she'd collapse to the ground exhausted by this journey, trying to be strong and independent but feeling so very alone.

"What about Jaci?" Justin asked quietly, stopping Jena dead in her tracks. "What does she think about all this? What's she going to do?"

Jena whipped her head around. "She doesn't know and you can't tell her. Promise me you won't tell her."

"You mean you have the deadly cancer gene and you haven't told your identical twin sister who likely has it, too?" he chastised.

Like Jena would willfully, and with a total disregard for her sister's wellbeing, withhold potentially lifesaving information. "It's a genetic mutation and she knows I went for testing but asked me not to share the result. And I respect that. She knows her risk is the same as mine and she's chosen regular cancer screening for early detection."

"Which makes perfect sense." Justin threw his hands up in the air.

"For her," Jena stressed. "She hasn't had three cancer scares in four years. She's not a mother. Maybe when she has children she'll change her mind, maybe she won't. It's *her* choice. And when our girls turn eighteen, I plan to be around to discuss their choices, as a living example that a strong family history of breast cancer and positive genetic testing isn't a death sentence, as a role model for taking control and seeking options. I will help them get the most up-to-date medical and treatment information. Then I'll support their decision regarding how they want to proceed." So they didn't have to go it alone like she had.

"If you wanted to keep the surgery quiet, why come home? Why not do it in South Carolina or anywhere but here?"

Because she needed to give Jaci time to get accustomed to caring for her nieces and make sure she'd be comfortable with the role of guardian. And she needed to be close by in case something went wrong with the surgery so Jaci could assume the responsibility immediately. "Some of the best doctors and hospitals in the world are within an hour of here. My doctor, who I trust implicitly, is here." Jena turned to pick up her sweater. "Now if you'll excuse me."

"No," Justin said. "I won't excuse you." He joined her in the entryway, crossed his arms over his chest and leaned his shoulder against the door, looking like he had no intention of moving any time soon. "So far you've been doing the majority of the talking and now I'd like a turn."

Jena took her watch out of her pocket and checked the time.

"Jaci and or Mandy will take care of the twins if they wake up. Now answer me this," he said. "What happens to *our* daughters if something goes horribly wrong during your surgery and you don't survive? Don't look at me like that. You're a nurse, you know all about complications and surgical risks. Don't tell me they hadn't crossed your mind."

Of course they had. The risks and benefits of going through with the surgeries had been clogging her mind for months. Day and night. "I've had legal documents drawn up, signed and witnessed in the presence of my attorney. If I should become incapacitated, Jaci has my power of attorney and can make decisions on my behalf. If I should…," thinking about it was bad enough but saying it out loud, actually hearing the words was excruciatingly difficult, she cleared her throat, "die, everything I have goes to the girls and the girls go to Jaci who's agreed if anything happens to me she'll adopt them and love them, provide for them, and raise them as close to how I would want them raised as she can manage." Although she didn't know it, Jena had left a guide of very detailed instructions with her attorney.

"Unacceptable," Justin yelled.

"You have no say," Jena yelled back.

"Now that's where you're wrong." He lowered his voice and narrowed his eyes. "I may not have a say in how you treat your body, but I most certainly have a say in the lives of *my* daughters, and I refuse to allow

you to put me in a position where I have to fight someone for custody."

Jena grabbed the kitchen counter for support. "I
didn't think you'd—"

He leaned in, angry, crowding her. Jena took a step
back. "Because apparently *you* don't know *me* all that
well, either. I'm not the boy you knew in high school.
I'm a responsible adult, and I am determined to do
what's best for *our* daughters, which is why you *will*
marry me and you'll do it *before* your surgery."

"But—"

"This isn't about you or me, Jena. This is about doing
what's best for Abbie and Annie. It's about them settling
in here and getting comfortable with me, and me learning to take care of them before, God forbid something
happens to you, so they'll have the stability of familiar surroundings and at least one parent in their lives."

Justin made sense, and she'd be lying if she didn't
admit a teeny tiny part of her may have, in private and
without her permission, hoped for this very outcome.
But, "There's no way—"

"You need to get married. I want to marry you. Why
are you making this so difficult? Do you find me so
objectionable—?"

"If you'd let me finish," Jena interrupted him. "Regardless of what either of us wants, there's no way we'll
be able to get married before my surgery."

Justin stood totally still. Watched her. Understanding dawned. "It's already scheduled. How? You just got
your money back. You have no insurance. And how did
you plan to sneak off and have the surgery without Jaci
finding out?"

"The Piermont name carries a lot of clout here in

Westchester County," Jena explained. "I met with my doctors, their staff, and representatives from the hospital who agreed to wait for payment of their exorbitant private pay rates until my birthday."

"Rather confident you'd find a husband," Justin pointed out.

Jena shared the harsh, disgusting truth. "Money can buy almost anything." Even a man willing to marry a fake-boobed mother of two. "Anyway, as for keeping it from Jaci, while working for Jerald, I've planned parties and coordinated rooms at all the major hotels in the area. And I handled all the scheduling of my mother's care. A quick couple of phone calls and I had a two room suite courtesy of the Piermont Enterprises account." She smiled. Her rat of a brother owed her. "And a nurse to stay with me and the girls for two weeks."

"What'd you tell Jaci?"

Nothing yet. She hated lying to her sister. It was too hard to think of saying good bye, telling her everything that needed to be said in case…

As if he understood her anguish he didn't wait for an answer. "When?"

"Wednesday." In two days.

Justin pulled out a chair from under the kitchen table and sat down. "So soon."

Two. Days.

Jena made the short distance between the counter and the kitchen table on numb legs, pulled out a chair and inelegantly plopped onto it. After weeks of fending off their attacks, doubt and indecision fought through her thin protective layer of certainty that surgery ASAP was the right path to take. Instead of being proactive was she actually being over-reactive? But the same argument against waiting waged a counter attack. Aunt Lynnie's breast cancer was diagnosed at stage III at age twenty-five, which Jena would turn in too short a time. Were the deadly mutant cells already multiplying inside her body? Was she already too late? Was she going to ruin her physical appearance and her sex life and her chance at a real marriage, real love, only to be stricken down by the disease anyway?

Justin eyed her with concern. "We're going to get through this," he said. So sure. So Confident.

Jena wanted to place her palms on some part of his body to draw on his strength to replenish her depleted reserves. She looked up at him. "We?" She wasn't his problem. This wasn't his concern. Jena would handle it on her own, like she handled everything else.

He placed his hand, palm up, on the table, stared into her eyes and waited.

She needed to touch him, feel him, absorb his certainty of a positive outcome, so she placed her hand in his larger one which he tightened around her. For some reason the gesture gave her hope, made her feel safe and protected.

"My mom left when I was two," Justin said, looking at the table as if remembering. "When I was old enough to understand, Grandma Abbie told me it was because my dad didn't take care of my mom the way she needed to be taken care of. I remember telling her when I grew up I'd do such a good job of taking care of my wife she'd never leave me. And I'd take such good care of my kids they'd love me forever. Grandma Abbie smiled," and so did he at the memory, "patted my head and called me a good boy." He shifted his gaze to their joined hands, loosened his grip, and ran his thumb back and forth over the backs of her fingers.

"Then Grandma Abbie died, leaving me alone with my dad for so many years, and I forgot my promise to her. As I grew I started following dad's egocentric example, becoming more and more like him each year. Oh I'd tell myself I was a better person. A better man. That given the chance I would be a better husband and father. Then, like on some subconscious level I thought myself incapable, I never let any woman get close enough for anything resembling a relationship so I wouldn't fail." He looked up.

"Then you came along and gave me two beautiful daughters who each share a part of us. Never have I wanted to do the right thing as much as I do now. You're my chance, Jena." He added his other hand hers in both of his. "To prove I'm a better man than my dad. To prove I'm worthy of being a husband and a father. That I'm capable of taking care of a family the right way. The way I'd promised my Grandma Abbie I would. The way you and the girls deserve. Let me, Jena. Give me that chance. Marry me."

Jena's eyes watered at his heartfelt words. She wanted so much to say yes. But the thought of Justin looking at her with the distaste and regret she'd seen in her father's eyes when he'd looked at his wife's post-surgical body kept her quiet.

"Say something," Justin prompted.

She couldn't.

"You okay?" he asked, squeezing her hand.

No. She was so far from okay she doubted they were even in the same time zone. "I need time to think." She yanked her hand from his and stood. "And you need to get ready for work." She hurried toward the door. "We can talk about this later." And she ran from his condo like the coward she was.

Later that night, after a hellacious shift on his day job, and a stop at a jewelry store after his ten hour day, Justin returned home to his quiet condo hungry, dirty and exhausted, yet determined to convince Jena to marry him despite the niggling apprehension that'd cropped up during the day. He threw his keys on the counter noticing one of Jena's amazing chocolate cakes sitting on an elegant crystal plate at the center of his kitchen table. He picked up the card beside it and read the inscription out loud, "Sorry I missed your birthday. Hope it was happy. If you're hungry when you get home I made you a meatloaf. It's in the refrigerator. Jena."

Not the "Yes I'll marry you" he'd hoped for, but thoughtful and appreciated. With all she had going on she'd taken time out of her day to cook for him. Because, he'd realized over the past couple of days, that's what Jena did. She took care of others. And while he considered himself fortunate to be on the receiving end of her caring, he couldn't help but wonder who took care of her?

Fifteen minutes later, showered and changed, Justin sat down to dinner and an ice cold beer. He took a forkful of actual home-cooked meal into his mouth, closed his eyes, and almost wept with joy. Man she could cook!

His hesitation toward marriage eased a bit. Hoping to alleviate it further—believing knowledge is power—Justin pushed his plate to the side and reached for his laptop, needing to learn about Jena's genetic condition, the surgical procedure she would be undergoing and the care she'd need afterward. And while he was at it, he hoped gain some understanding as to what would drive a perfectly healthy young woman to undergo a drastic body-altering surgery that carved off a female's most prominent, identifiable and let's be honest, arousable attributes of her sexual identity.

Once booted up he typed in keyword: breast cancer gene. Over the next three hours he added BRCA2, mother with breast cancer, dense breasts cancer risk, treatment breast cancer, survival rates breast cancer, and prophylactic bilateral mastectomies to his search.

He scanned dozens of articles, both technical medical pieces and detailed personal accountings from women, some Jena's age, a few in various stages of dealing with cancer others recovering from prophylactic bilateral mastectomies. And blogs. With pictures. He could have done without the pictures. Yet some unknown force had compelled him to look.

By the time he shut down his computer Justin had a newfound understanding of Jena's plight and acceptance of her plan. But thanks to the pictures, he also had a newfound concern over whether he actually possessed the strength of character necessary to give Jena what she would need to help her through recovery and dealing with the altered body image he'd read about. He shook his head to scatter the images now plaguing him. Scarred, unnatural, irregularly shaped mounds. Without nipples.

Suddenly Jena's willingness to marry a gay man made sense, to avoid rejection from a straight man. A man like Justin.

Would he still be attracted to her after surgery? Would his body respond to her in the same way it did now? God help him, what if he wasn't? What if it didn't? What if he couldn't?

Idiot. He smacked both palms on the table, the burn bringing his focus where it belonged. This wasn't about sex and it wasn't about him. It was about Jena, the mother of his daughters, an integral member of their four person family unit. And the tremendous respect he had for her strength in making what had to be an excruciatingly difficult decision meant to prolong her life in the face of a well-documented, very real, and significantly elevated risk of developing cancer.

A decision he'd belittled by making it about breast removal, when it was really about so much more. Selfish jerk.

Her words haunted him. *As long as I have the choice, I choose life. And if choosing life means I have to live it without a pair of breasts and a uterus, then so be it.* And, *I am more than a pair of breasts.*

Yes she was. Jena Piermont was a dedicated, loving mother, an amazingly strong, courageous woman who he'd be lucky and honored to have as a wife. And he couldn't wait until morning to tell her. He picked up his cell phone to check the time. Ten thirty-one. He didn't want to wake her or the babies. So he dialed Ian.

"Hey," he said when Ian answered. "What's going on down there?"

"Well, Jaci's out of her mind with worry about Jena. She's been pacing back and forth and talking to herself for the past half hour."

"Who's on the phone?" Jaci asked in the background. "Is that Justin? Give me the phone."

"Good luck," Ian said. Then Jaci came on. "Justin

Rangore you had better tell me what's going on with my sister or our friendship is over."

"Hi, Jaci."

"Don't you 'Hi, Jaci' me all friendly like nothing's wrong. Jena's gone quiet. She barely said two words since Ian and I got home from work. From the looks of my condo and my refrigerator she's been cooking and cleaning all day, typical upset Jena behavior. She served us this elaborate feast for dinner then disappeared into her room without eating a bite. Something's going on and I know you know what it is."

Yeah, he did. And as much as he'd like to confide in Jaci and or Ian, his two closest friends, he couldn't. "I'm coming down," Justin said, disconnecting the call before Jaci could protest. Then he retrieved the engagement ring he'd bought for Jena—because even if they couldn't marry before her surgery, at least they could be officially engaged. And his emergency key to Jaci's condo—in case she went all angry and refused to open the door. And one, no, three condoms—because he was a guy and guys always remained hopeful, and therefore, should always be prepared.

Too impatient to wait for the elevator he took the stairs down. To find Ian casually leaning with his back to the hallway wall beside Jaci's door, waiting for him. "I'm supposed to stop you from coming in," he said half-joking when Justin reached him.

"You going to try?" If he wanted a fight Justin would give him one.

"Nah." He held up two fingers. "On two conditions."

"Name them."

"One, you look me in the eyes and promise me that

you talking to Jena right now is going to make things better and not worse."

Justin looked him in the eyes. "I promise." At least he hoped.

"Two, you give me some bit of information to relay to Jaci so she'll calm down enough for me to get her into bed." Ian smiled. "I'll take it from there."

Justin reached into his pocket, took out the velvet ring box he'd stashed there, and opened the lid to expose the two-carat emerald cut diamond ring, the sales lady assured him Jena would love, inside. She damn well better for all it cost him. "Tell Jaci, I'm here to propose to Jena." And to let Jena know he supported her decision to opt for surgery and would stand by her and take care of her and the girls. His family. That she wasn't alone.

Ian held out his hand to shake Justin's. "Congratulations, man." Their hands clasped together, Ian jerked Justin forward and they bumped shoulders in a male sort of hug.

"I need a favor," Justin said when they parted. "You okay with moving out so I can move Jena and the girls upstairs with me tomorrow?"

Ian smiled. "What's your rush?"

If only Justin could tell him. "You okay with that or not? You're sleeping down here every night anyway."

"Tomorrow night work?" Ian asked as he slowly pushed open the door.

"The earlier the better."

Ian looked back. "Keep it down," he whispered. "Mandy and Maddie are asleep in the living room. Jena's door is closed. Not sure what she's doing but there's no noise coming from her room so I'm guessing the twins are asleep."

By the light over the kitchen sink, Justin followed Ian into the condo and down the hall to Jena's room. He knocked lightly. She didn't answer. He tried the doorknob. Unlocked. So he turned it and as quiet as he could so he didn't wake the twins, pushed into the dark room. "Jena?" he whispered.

A lamp lit up in the far corner of the crowded room revealing two cribs end to end along one wall, a changing table and bureau along another. A laundry basket of folded pink and yellow baby clothes sat on the floor. Two car seats lay stacked one on top of the other in a corner. Two baby swings. Two lay on the floor and play with the dangling thingies things. And hardly any room to move.

"Justin?" Jena whispered. "Is something wrong?"

Their cramped living area for one thing. "Where did all this stuff come from?"

"I wanted to make the condo look nice for Ian and Jaci so I moved all of Abbie and Annie's stuff in here so everyone would stop tripping over it."

She sat up in the bed her hair a mess, her eyes puffy and rimmed in red, the tip of her nose a dark pink and asked, "What are you doing here?"

"I've spent the last couple of hours on the computer doing research, which is why I'm down here so late. Sorry about that, by the way."

"No problem," she said, looking at him. Wary. "What did you research?"

"The breast cancer gene. Breast cancer in general. Prophylactic bilateral mastectomies."

She threw her pretty, bare legs over the side of the bed. "If you came down here to try to talk me out of—"

He sat down beside her. "I came down to tell you I am humbled by your courage."

She stared at him with watery blue eyes.

"I can't imagine what it must be like to be in your situation, and if I were, I don't know if I'd have the balls to do what you're planning to do." He took her small hands into his, brought them to his lips and kissed her knuckles. "There's no one I would rather have as a role model for our daughters than you. They need you. *We* need you. And selfish man that I am, I want you to take advantage of whatever treatment will enable you to remain here on earth with us for as long as possible."

Tears spilled out of the corners of both of her eyes.

"You were right," he said, feeling somewhat choked up himself. "You are so much more than a pair of breasts. You're the mother of my children, a woman I care about, a woman who matters to me."

She reached for a tissue and dabbed at her nose. "Thank you. But—"

"No buts." Justin stood, pulled the ring box from his pocket and went down on one knee. "I don't know what the future will bring." He flipped open the lid and tilted the sparkly diamond in her direction. "I *do* know that I want you, me, Abbie and Annie to be a family, a real, traditional family that lives together and takes care of one another. Not to be a complete cornball, but in sickness and in health, in good times and in bad." He looked up at her and tilted his head. "You want me to keep going?"

She gave him a small, almost shy smile and shook her head.

"So what do you say, Jena? Will you marry me?"

The smile faded.

"Before you answer there's something I think you should know," he started out, hoping to make a point. "It's not easy keeping this physique in tip top shape. And with me being a family man and all I doubt I'll have much time to get to the gym." He stuck out his belly and patted it. "Based on tonight's sampling of your culinary skills, I'm thinking there's a real good chance if you marry me you may be taking on a future three-hundred-pounder. You willing to marry me knowing that in the months and years to come my body may look totally different than it looks right now?"

More tears leaked out of her eyes. But she gifted him with a small nod.

"Are you willing to marry me, *knowing* that my body *will* soon look and feel different than it does right now?" she asked in a soft voice.

He stared into her eyes. "Yes." He removed the ring from the box and held it out to her. "Jena Piermont, will you do me the honor of becoming my wife."

While she thought about it Justin's heart proved it is actually possible for a heart to beat against a ribcage. Or at least feel that way.

"I'll accept your ring," she said slowly, looking down at him. "I'll agree to get engaged on one condition."

"Anything."

"If, after my surgery, you find me…unattractive…"

"I won't," he said, meaning it, wanting it, praying he could manage it.

She looked away. "And you don't want to…"

"Jena," he said. "Look at me." She turned her head slowly. "Let's get through the surgery first. The rest we'll deal with as it comes up."

"But I want you to promise to be honest with me. To

talk to me about what you're thinking and feeling. And if you change your mind about marrying me it's okay."

"I won't change my mind," he tried to reassure her.

But she went on like he hadn't even spoken. "I couldn't bear you being unhappy, or turning your back on me in bed, or looking at me with revulsion and regret."

Her distress affected him, made him desperate to comfort her. "I promise to be honest with you. But I won't—"

She placed to fingers on his lips to quiet him. "Thank you. That's all I needed to hear." Then she held out her hand and he slid the engagement ring onto her finger.

She lifted her hand up to the light. "This is the most beautiful ring I've ever seen." He doubted that. "I love it." Whew. "It fits perfectly. How did you…?"

"I held the hand of every woman in the store until I found one that fit like yours."

Justin's cell phone went off. He grabbed it to silence the ringtone and looked at the screen. "It's your sister." He held the phone out to Jena.

"She knows?"

"I had to come clean to Ian about my intentions or he threatened not to let me in. But she doesn't know your answer. And since she'll probably come barging in here any minute if you don't tell her…"

Jena took the phone. "Hi, Jaci. Yes, Justin proposed." She smiled. "Yes, I said yes." Jaci screamed loud enough to startle one of the babies. "Shshsh," Jena said. Then she looked up at him, uncertain and said into the phone, "I don't know. Definitely by our birthday."

Justin leaned forward. "But we're moving in together tomorrow." Because his future wife needed him to take care of her and their daughters. He said a quick prayer that he'd be able to do a decent job of it.

"Perfect," Jena said to Jaci. Then, "Now I've got to go. Justin's pawing at my pajamas."

He wasn't but took that as his cue to start.

One of the babies made some sucking noises. Shoot. "How long do we have until they wake up?" he asked, lifting Jena's silky pink negligée over her head. "Love this, by the way."

Jena removed his shirt. "Probably around fifteen minutes." She grabbed his hand and yanked him onto the bed. "Longer if you keep real quiet and you let me turn off the light," she teased.

"Longer is good." He slid her pink lacy panties down to her ankles while she reached for the lamp. "For the record, I am a huge fan of sexy lingerie."

She pulled him down on top of her and whispered, "So am I."

CHAPTER EIGHT

JENA should have added "Frontal lobotomy" to her enormous list of Things To Do The Day Before Surgery, because adding "Move in with Justin", "Cancel hotel reservation and nurse", and "Change will to make Justin the sole legal guardian of the girls" showed a severe decision-making impairment in need of immediate remediation.

But at least she'd kept so busy she hadn't had time to worry and obsess. Which meant she'd probably be up most of the night.

"One slippery baby fresh from the bath." Jena lifted Abbie from her baby tub and handed her into the pink towel draped over Justin's arms. "You have her?"

"I have her." Justin cuddled Abbie close with one hand and wrapped the towel and hood around her with the other. Careful and gentle. The ideal parent.

Jena spread the yellow towel on the bathmat then lifted Annie out of her tub, wrapped her in the yellow towel, and lifted the squirmy baby into her arms.

"You're sure you're ready to go solo?" she asked on the way to the second bedroom.

"Gotta try sometime."

Except for leaving for a few hours to complete the paperwork necessary to take an emergency two-week leave of absence from work, Justin had been by her side all day. Watching. Learning. Helping. She couldn't have asked for more in a fiancé.

"Be a good girl for daddy," Jena said shaking Abbie's little foot through the towel.

Justin smiled. Seemed he liked being called daddy. Which made Jena smile, too.

"Time to get you ready for bed," he said, placing Abbie on the changing table. "And you and your sister better sleep for a good couple of hours because daddy has special plans for mommy tonight."

Since they only had one changing table, Jena set Annie on the bed. "Oh does he?" she asked, an excited tingle taking up residence deep in her core. There was nothing she'd rather do than spend the night before her surgery in Justin's arms. Every night in his arms.

"What the—?" Justin said. "That is not being good for daddy."

Jena looked at the changing table, watched Justin rush to cover Abbie's privates with her towel and laughed. "You've got to be quick."

"She got everything wet," he complained.

"I'll clean it up when we're done," she said. "Come. Join me on the bed."

He looked over his shoulder. "Why, Jena. I'd love to join you on the bed." He wiggled his eyebrows.

"To finish changing Abbie," she specified.

"Spoilsport."

He grabbed the baby wipes, a diaper, rash cream, and a new set of pink PJs and moved to the bed. "No more funny business," he ordered, setting Abbie on the bed next to Annie.

And in typical fashion, while Annie lay quietly,

Abbie started to squirm. He handed her a rattle. Then he got started, concentrating so intensely, Jena didn't think he even realized he was talking himself through it as he went. "Diaper, tabs in the back. Check. Shoot. Clean with a baby wipe first." He did a very thorough job. "*Then* diaper, tabs in the back. Check. Diaper rash cream. Yuk." He wiped his fingers on the towel. "Cover her up. Check. Secure sticky tabs. Check. Yes!" He lifted his hands over his head in victory. "Job well done."

Jena laughed again. Changing the girls had never been this entertaining.

Justin struggled to insert Abbie's kicking feet into the leg openings of her sleeper. "Minor setback." Out of the corner of her eye she caught him watching her. "You make it look so easy. Some trick of the hands for sure."

Abbie started to cry.

"Shshshsh. We don't want mommy to think daddy's incompetent."

Jena smiled. And fell in love with him, trying so hard to do a good job of taking care of his daughter.

"You're far from incompetent," she reassured him. "I've been doing this a lot longer than you have. And I've learned it's easier to hold the leg like this." She took a firm but gentle hold of Annie's leg over her knee. "Then put the sleeper on over the leg rather than trying to put the leg into the sleeper. Does that make sense?"

Justin followed her lead and had Abbie dressed in under a minute. "Works for flailing arms, too."

That it did.

With both babies dressed they moved to the kitchen where Jena supervised Justin making and heating up bottles like she'd taught him earlier, while she held the girls.

Again he concentrated on doing everything exactly as she'd shown him and spoke out loud as he did it. "Take the plastic insert like this—don't touch the inside. And only use bottled water at room temperature." He lifted the jug and poured a measured amount into each bottle. "I measure the powdered formula carefully according to the instructions on the can." Which he double checked. "And I don't change brands without checking with the doctor first." He looked and Jena and she nodded. "I replace the ring and cap and shake." He did.

"Then I unscrew the ring and remove the nipple before placing the bottle in the microwave." He set the microwave as she'd taught him and pressed start. "After heating, I reattach the ring, shake again to eliminate any hot spots, then squeeze out any remaining air into the sink like this."

Abbie arched her back and screamed her displeasure at the formula not being squirted into her mouth.

"Then, even though my daughters are ravenous and crying loud enough to make the neighbors think we're abusing them, which makes me feel like a terrible parent because I am taking so long, I don't, under any circumstances, feed them until I check the temperature of each bottle by squeezing a small amount of formula on the inside of my wrist, like this." He demonstrated.

"Perfect," Jena said when he'd finished. "Now take your daughter." She handed him Abbie, who had become quite the daddy's girl.

Justin smiled proudly. "I feel like I just aced an important test."

"Care to join me on the couch?" she asked. An innocent enough invitation. But Jena's mind wandered to the last time they'd come together on that couch. Both naked with her straddling his lap.

He looked at her with a teasing grin. "Based on that cute blush of yours, you are so thinking what I'm thinking."

Busted.

"To feed our daughters," she clarified because it seemed they both required clarification.

Jena settled into the couch and gave Annie the bottle. Justin must have given Abbie her bottle at the same time because instant quiet. Ahhhhh. "This is my favorite part of the day," Jena said. The peacefulness of sitting in a darkened room, while holding her sleepily relaxed, contentedly sucking daughter or daughters.

"I can see why," Justin said. "But my goal as your future husband will be to make *our* bedtime your favorite part of the day."

If she survived the surgery. If they continued to share a bed. If he wasn't completely turned off by the post- surgical changes in her body. Quick, change the subject. "It's so nice to have help, so each of our daughters can get the individual cuddling she deserves," she said. "Abbie's a gulper so you need to be diligent about burping her after each ounce. No matter how much she protests."

And boy did she protest. "I think this one's going to be trouble," Justin said trying to hold Abbie still while he patted her back.

"Maybe," Jena said calmly. "And if she is, we'll handle it. But please promise me you won't label her. The troublemaker. The wild one. People used to label Jaci and me as a way of telling us apart. We both hated that. And you know what? For as long as I can remember, people called Jaci 'The Wild One.' Since we were little girls. And she did, in fact, grow up to be 'The Wild One.' Was it because she was born that way or was she simply living up to what people expected of her?"

"If I had my guess I'd say she was born that way. But I get your point. No labels. Promise."

As the girls drifted off to sleep Jena and Justin sat side by side in companionable silence, until Jena's thoughts turned to her surgery and dozens of unpleasant "what if" scenarios. She needed to move around, to work off some of the accumulating nervous energy and keep her mind busy. So she stood. "I'm tired and I still have to clean up."

"Hopefully you're not *too* tired," Justin said as he stood, too.

She wasn't.

He followed her to the cribs and set Abbie down, gently, on her side, with a rolled blanket at her back and a light comforter covering her, exactly as she'd shown him for their nap earlier.

On his way out, he brushed past her, sliding his front along her back and his chin along her curls. As he passed he whispered, "I'll do the kitchen. Then I'll be waiting for you in our bedroom."

Jena almost melted.

She cleaned up the girls' room and the bathroom on auto-pilot, having done it so often she barely paid attention anymore, even in her new environment. Her thoughts filled with tomorrow and what she had to do beforehand. Show Justin the notebook where she'd written down the girls' routines, likes and dislikes, and important information/telephone numbers. Add Abbie and Annie's birth certificates and her updated will. She'd kept Jaci as her Health Care Proxy, couldn't risk Justin shutting down life support prematurely if he changed his mind and decided he wanted to be rid of her. Oh, and she couldn't forget to put out the letters she'd written, just in case.

With the bathroom clean, Jena clipped up her hair and jumped into the shower, wanted tonight to be perfect. But when she stepped out and caught a glimpse of her naked reflection in the mirror she couldn't look away from the sight of her body with two full, beautiful, real breasts. She cupped them, their weighted fullness heavy in her palms. She ran her thumbs over her dark nipples, felt them tighten and the responding needy twinge that traveled all the way down to between her legs. Always so sensitive, so arousing.

The impending loss burned through her. The finality of it. Complete. Permanent.

Cleaning up the kitchen and lighting the three dozen candles he'd placed around his bedroom took Justin all of ten minutes.

Now what?

He went into the master bathroom to wash up and brush his teeth.

Fifteen minutes down.

He stripped off his clothes and pulled on a pair of black satin boxer shorts.

Sixteen minutes.

How long did it take Jena to get ready for bed? At twenty-five minutes he went looking for her, finding the door to the hall bathroom partially closed. He peered through the crack to see her, staring at her naked torso in the large mirror over the sink, tracing the shape of her exquisite breasts with her fingers, looking sad.

He knocked softly as he pushed open the door.

She didn't flinch or move to cover herself, mesmerized by her reflection. "I'm saying goodbye," she said.

Justin walked up behind her, covered her hands with his, and leaned down to whisper in her ear. "Come to bed so we can say goodbye together."

"In a minute," she said.

Yeah right. She'd already had twenty-five minutes.

"Thank you for today." She looked at him via the mirror. "For taking time off from your job and working so hard to learn the girls' routines and get us settled in. I really appreciate it."

And he appreciated her giving him the opportunity to step up and do the right thing. "You're welcome." He caressed her breasts and now her hands rested on top of his. She closed her eyes and let her head drop back to his collar bone, elongating her neck.

"I've been thinking." He bent to dot a line of kisses down the side of her neck. "I've decided it's time for me to find a new favorite female body part," he said. "Breasts are so yesterday." He moved his hands to her hips, kissed back up her neck and dipped his tongue into the small cove at the base of her ear.

She tilted her head to give him better access and moaned.

"I think this is the spot. The delicate curve of a woman's neck." He kissed his way back down. "*My* woman's neck," he specified.

"Perfect," she said on an aroused sigh.

Perfect indeed.

"Now come," he prompted.

"In a minute, I promise." She moved his hands and gave him a gentle shove toward the door. "I want to make myself pretty for you."

"The clock starts now," he turned her, kissed her lips, and pressed his growing erection against her. "I can't wait much longer."

A few minutes later she stood in the doorway to his, no their, bedroom looking at all the candles and every second he'd waited had been worth it. Speech eluded him. Never in all his days had he seen a vision lovelier than Jena at that moment in time, her loose curls teasing at the thin straps of a pale pink, knee-length silk negligee with a deep, tantalizing V that dipped between her breasts and two sexy side slits that showed off plenty of leg. On her feet she wore a pair of silver stilettoes which matched the silver earrings dangling from her ears. He met her at the door. "You are…stunning."

"The room looks beautiful all lit up with candles."

Especially for her. He knew she'd like it. "*You* look beautiful." And alluring. And his. And he wanted her. Now.

"Thank you," she said. "And thank you for going out of your way to make this night special." She leaned in to kiss his cheek, her silky body pressed to his, her aroused nipples poking his chest. He refused to think about her surgery and changes that may or may not occur in their sex life as a result. Because right now he had his sexy fiancée in his arms and nothing would keep him from making this night off the charts amazing.

He backed her toward the bed. "You smell so good." Fragrant. Floral. Enticing.

"You feel so good." She ran her soft hands up his

chest, over his shoulders then down his arms. "So strong." She set a soft, sweet kiss on his right pectoral.

He pulled her close reveled in the feel of her, thread his fingers through her hair, angled her head so he could plant a lusty kiss on her luscious lips. On contact a potent arousal surged through his system. His body hardened in response. "You drive me wild, Jena Piermont." He kissed her again, slid his tongue into the slick heat of her mouth, over and over until he needed to break for air. "I want to take things slow, to linger and make tonight last, but I don't know if I can."

"I don't want slow right now." She pushed down his boxers which dropped to the floor at his feet. "Save it for next time." She cupped him and he almost finished before he'd started.

He moved her hand, lifted her negligee over her head and followed her down to the bed where he lavished attention on her breasts. Caressed them, kissed them, squeezed and sucked and loved them. And said his goodbyes before moving down to the elastic of her panties. "These have to go." He shimmied down to her ankles with them and slid them over her sexy heels before kissing his way back up. "Open for me." She bent her knees and dropped each to the side so he could get to her inner thighs. Higher.

She moaned and writhed and clutched his head tightly as he tasted and enjoyed her. "Please," she begged. "I need you." She pulled his hair. "Make love to me. Now."

They were of one mind. He crawled on top of her, not taking the time to expose the fancy new sheets he'd bought for her, reached for a condom and rolled it on. He positioned himself for entry. "Are you ready?"

"I feel like I've been waiting for this moment my entire life."

Oddly enough, "Me, too." He nudged her entrance, found her wet and ready, and thrust into her tight, slick heat. She wrapped her arms and legs around him, contracted her muscles, and squeezed him inside and out. Fully ensconced. The sensation wonderful. Astounding. So. Damn. Good. "My, God, Jena. You feel so unbelievably fantastic. I'm afraid if I move I'll—"

She rocked her hips and that was it. Justin thrust into her, over and over, got lost in her depths, went out of his mind with lust. "You feel so good, baby." He kissed her. Felt a connection, more than sex. Caring. He wanted to please her, to make her happy, to make her love him. Pressure started to build. He needed release. But not without her. He slipped a hand between them.

"Oh my heavens that feels good," Jena cried out, panting and rocking into his touch.

Oh my heavens. Only Jena. He smiled.

She dug her fingers into his back, clamped her legs about his butt, and urged him deeper. "Yes."

He fought for control. Needed to wait. "Come on, baby. Come for me." Now. Please.

She tightened around him.

He rode out her orgasm then let go, his release powerfully satisfying. On a scale of one to ten, a twenty-five, with an intensity people dream of, but few are ever lucky enough to achieve.

"Goodness gracious, I love you," Jena said dreamily on a long, contented sigh.

The aftereffects of best-sex-ever talking. But it got Justin thinking of how nice it would be to be loved by Jena. To hold hands and cuddle on the couch, to know that his safe return home from work mattered to someone and over dinner that same someone was eager to engage in conversation about his and her day. He rolled to the side, taking her with him, still joined together, and held her close. He kissed her forehead, realizing he wanted her to love him. And he wanted to love her and for their marriage to be real and happy and not only for the sake of their children or to gain release of a trust fund.

CHAPTER NINE

A FEW short hours later, after a night of loving Jena
would never forget, it was time to go. She looked around
the condo wondering if this was the last time she'd ever
see it. Justin's stomach growled. "You're silly for not
eating breakfast," she said.

To which he replied, "Like I already told you, if you
can't eat I'm not going to eat."

Too sweet.

He pushed the double stroller out the door to head
up to Mrs. Calvin's, who'd agreed to watch the girls
overnight. Jena popped her head out the door and said,
"I'll meet you upstairs. There's one more thing I need
to do." She pulled each of the four letters she'd written,
just in case, out of her folder. She sorted through them
once again to check that they were all there. One for
Jaci. One for Abbie. One for Annie. And one for Justin. Each sealed with a lipstick kiss. She kissed each
one again for good measure and set them on the kitchen
table. "God willing you'll never have to read them."

Justin drove Jena to the hospital where he accompanied her to the plastic surgeon's office to get marked
prior to surgery. Then he remained by her side, holding
her hand, his presence calming and reassuring, until
the nurse denied him access to the surgical suite. He

leaned over the railing on the stretcher, kissed her on the lips and whispered. "I am not leaving this hospital without you."

A few minutes later, as the anesthesiologist administered her medication, while she counted back from fifty, Jena thought about Justin's last loving kiss and his emotion-filled expression as he told her, "*I am not leaving this hospital without you*" and felt at peace.

Jena emerged from sedation unable to move but aware of sounds. A monitor beeped out a steady rhythm. People talked, Justin and a male voice she didn't recognize. She tried to open her eyes but couldn't. She swallowed. Her mouth felt dry.

She drifted back to sleep.

The next time she awoke to quiet, lying on a bed. This time she opened her eyes to a darkened hospital room. A big, warm hand held hers. She turned her head. Justin stared back at her. "About time," he said with a smile.

"I made it." She forced a small smile. "Time?" It hurt to talk.

"Nine o'clock at night."

"Water?"

He stood to get a cup and held a straw at her mouth. She took a small sip.

"Abbie and Annie?"

"Mrs. Calvin says they're doing fine. One of her granddaughters came over after school and is spending the night to help her. She said not to worry about a thing and to concentrate on healing."

Jena tried to change her position, felt an uncomfortable pull beneath her armpit, and winced.

"Should I buzz for the nurse?" Justin asked. Worried. "Do you need pain medication?"

"No. Feel strange. Woozy."

He sat down. "The doctor said to expect you to be groggy."

"You don't have to stay," she said.

"I know I don't *have* to. I *want* to stay." He leaned in close. "Maybe you don't remember, but I told you earlier. I'm not leaving this hospital without you."

She thought that'd been a dream. "Okay by me." Jena closed her eyes and drifted back to sleep.

The next afternoon Justin walked beside Jena ready to catch her, amazed she'd made it from the car to the fifth floor unassisted. "I can't believe you refused to stay in the hospital another night," he said. He'd even offered to pay for the room, not that she needed his money.

"I'm fine," she said, but more tight-lipped than the last time she told him. "I need to be home."

"Almost there." Duh. Of course she knew they were almost there.

Justin wanted to help her, to hold her up but he didn't know where it was safe to touch her above the waist. In addition to two dressings over her breasts, held in place by a surgical bra he'd seen glimpses of, Jena had four bulb-type drains he'd been taught to empty, two below each armpit, that she said hurt worse than her surgical incisions.

In the condo, Justin got Jena settled into the recliner chair where she promptly fell asleep.

And for the first time since they'd left the hospital he inhaled deeply then exhaled a relieved breath. They'd made it. He entered the kitchen to microwave water for a cup of coffee and saw some letters on the table. Four of them.

He lifted the one on top labeled "Justin" and opened it.

Dear Justin,
If you're reading this letter I guess my worst fears
have been realized and I didn't survive the sur-
gery.

A read-if-I-die letter. He dropped it and hurried over to Jena—to check her breathing—fearing he'd somehow jinxed her by reading a letter she'd intended for post-mortem viewing. The thought made him sick to his stomach. The microwave pinged. He dumped the boiling water down the sink and sat at the table. Stared at the letter. Wondered what she'd want him to know if she wasn't here to tell him. Only she *was* here, thank you, God. And whatever she had to say to him he'd much rather hear coming from her beautiful lips in her melodic voice. He picked up the letter and crumbled it into a ball. But couldn't get himself to throw it out.

Curiosity got the better of him.

He flattened out the wrinkles.

I'm sorry to leave you alone to care for our daugh-
ters. You have to know if it were at all within my
power to be there with you, I would be. Since I'm
not, I thought you should know I have complete
confidence in your ability to raise our daughters
in a way that would make me proud. Don't be
afraid to ask for help if you need it.
In the pages that follow I've left detailed in-

structions for special things I'd like you to do for the girls each year, little things to help them remember me and how much I loved them.

Justin's heart felt raw and he reached for a napkin to blot his eye. This was crazy. He should be celebrating Jena's survival not reading this letter, but he had to know how it ended.

In high school, I had a crush on the boy you were, handsome, fearless, and fun. As an adult, it's only taken me a few short days to fall in love with the man you've become, still handsome, fearless and fun but also kind and gentle, confident and responsible. Your support and help has meant so much. Nothing would have made me happier than to live out my years as your wife. I am so sorry I didn't get the chance.
I love you.
Yours Always,
Jena

Justin sat back and clasped his hands behind his head. Jena loved him. He looked over at her sleeping form. Never in his life did he ever think it possible that a smart, proper, discriminating woman like Jena would ever see him as more than a quick screw. *I love you. Yours Always, Jena.* She loved him. Always.

And since his hours in the surgical waiting room consisted of some time spent considering the possibility of a life without Jena—during which his insides felt like every one of his internal organs had gone rotten—he was pretty sure he loved her right back. And he'd make it a point to tell her at the first opportunity. He glanced at the clock on the stove. An hour until dinner.

Time to prove his worth as a family man. He preheated the oven, took out the vegetable lasagna Jena had left in the refrigerator, and put it in to cook. Then he called Mrs. Calvin and went upstairs to retrieve the twins.

They started to cry in the elevator. Maybe he should have taken Mrs. Calvin up on her offer to feed them before he took them home. But in giving a full report on Jena's condition, he'd already spent more time upstairs than he'd planned, and he worried about leaving Jena alone for too long. "Daddy's going to take good care of you," he told them as he wheeled the stroller down the hallway. "You need to quiet down or you'll wake mommy."

Seems they were more concerned with their empty bellies.

He entered the condo ready to apologize for waking Jena, to find the recliner chair empty. "Jena," he called out, maneuvering the stroller inside and closing the door.

No answer.

He walked to the closed door of the hall bathroom. "Jena?" He tried the knob. Locked. "Jena!" He knocked on the door.

"I'm fine," she said, sounding weak.

"Unlock the door."

"Go take care of Abbie and Annie. I don't need any help."

"Call me if you do," he said. Although how the heck would he hear her over their crying daughters?

He rushed to get the bottles made. Had all his supplies lined up and was ready to start when he heard a horrible gassy squirty type noise come from the vicinity of the stroller. Red-faced Annie—dressed in yellow— the guilty party. "This is not a very good time," Justin said as he placed the empty liner-filled bottles on the counter to wheel the girls into their bedroom.

He picked up Annie, holding her away from him so her soiled bottom didn't leak onto him. He set her on the changing table. "Daddy will have you all cleaned up in a minute." He unsnapped her outfit, revealing her cubby legs. Then he undid the diaper and, "My, God!" He closed her back up. But not before a hideous odor wafted up to the pocket of air where his next inhaled breath had come from. He retched. While he may be new to this diaper changing thing, it did not take an expert to see that Annie was not tolerating her formula well and something needed to be done. He eased down the front of the diaper. Slowly. Hoping. Nope. That gag-worthy, hold-your-nose-and-close-your-eyes mess had not been his imagination. And it was, in fact, as bad as he'd first thought.

Annie kicked and twisted, and the mess started to spread.

"Whoa. Hold still."

She didn't.

"I can do this," Justin chanted. "I can do this." Had to do this. Like ripping off a Band-Aid. Do it quick. He turned his head, inhaled and removed the diaper. It took eight baby wipes and four gasps of tainted air to get her clean. He set her on a fresh towel, put on a new diaper and changed her into a sleeper. In what had to beat the slowest most toxic diaper change on record.

While Annie had calmed down, Abbie continued

to scream. He couldn't put Annie back in the stroller which she'd defiled, so he set her on the bed. Then got worried she'd roll off. Although he'd never seen her roll, and had no idea when she might start, he refused to risk it. She would not get hurt on his watch.

He put Annie in her crib—which she did not like at all, and ran to check on Jena.

He knocked on the closed bathroom door.

Nothing.

Abbie and Annie continued to scream their displeasure with him not giving them his full attention.

He pressed his ear to the door. "Jena? Are you okay?"

He heard what sounded like sobbing. "Go away." Her words, the way she said them, conveyed absolute misery.

"Open this door or I'm going to kick it in."

A smoke detector went off somewhere in the condo, the noise shrill, and loud enough to drown out Annie and Abbie. Something smelled burnt. Damn it. The lasagna. He ran to the kitchen and opened the oven door releasing a plume of thick black smoke. He turned on the fan over the stove. It did nothing. He checked for flames, seeing none he closed the oven door and turned it off.

He ran back to the bathroom. "Jena!" He pounded on the door.

But the girls were screaming and the smoke alarm blaring and now someone was knocking on his front door. He ran to open it to see his pain-in-the-ass neighbor. "It's okay. Burned dinner." He slammed the door in the man's face.

He climbed on a chair and tried to disable the smoke alarm.

He glanced at the closed bathroom door worried about Jena. Surely, if she was okay she'd have come out to investigate. The siren hurt his ears. The smoke made him cough. And Justin realized he could not handle this alone.

Don't be afraid to ask for help if you need it.

He hopped off the chair and called Jaci then ran to check on the girls to make sure the smoke hadn't affected them. He found a screaming Annie in her crib, her pink cheeks wet with tears, her legs kicking in anger. Abbie had gotten herself all wedged sideways in the stroller, pushing with her legs and jamming her head into the side cushion. And she had a cut under her eye. Tiny but a definite nick. With blood. "Dammit." He unstrapped her lucky she hadn't strangled herself. He was a total screw up. A failure at fatherhood. What the hell had he been thinking taking on care of an incapacitated Jena and two babies by himself?

"Justin," Jaci called out.

"In here."

He heard some banging and the smoke alarm went quiet.

Jaci entered the girls' bedroom followed by Ian who held a broom. Justin handed Abbie to Ian, picked up Annie from the crib and dragged Jaci by her arm to the bathroom. "I'm sorry to do this to you, and Jena will probably hate me forever, but I don't know if she needs a nurse or her sister. All I do know is she needs someone and she certainly isn't opening the door for me." He knocked. "Jaci's here. Open up."

"No," Jena cried out.

"What the hell did you do to her that she locked herself in the bathroom?" Ian asked.

"Shut up." Justin pushed Annie into Ian's other arm. "Go wait in my bedroom and open a window. I'll be in with the bottles in a minute."

Ian didn't move until Jaci said, "Go. The smoke isn't good for them."

"What happened?" Jaci asked, worried.

"She needs to be the one to tell you," Justin said. He leaned close to the door. "Honey, come on. It's me or Jaci. One of us is coming in." Tomorrow he'd remove the lock.

"Jena," Jaci said calmly through the door. "You're scaring me. Please, let me in."

The lock clicked. Thank you. Jaci turned the knob, opened the door and peered inside. She must have gotten the go ahead because she disappeared into the bathroom and closed the door behind her. Justin didn't have time to feel relieved because he still needed to tend to Abbie and Annie. So he headed to aerate the kitchen and make bottles.

Jena sat back down on the closed lid of the toilet, too tired to stand any longer, sore from wriggling out of her zip up sweat jacket and multiple unsuccessful attempts to empty her drains.

Jaci stood with her back to the door, staring down at Jena's surgical bra in shock. "What happened?" It didn't take her long to figure it out. "No," she whispered. Her eyes went wide and filled with tears. "Not cancer." She lifted her fingertips to her mouth. "Not you."

"I'm fine," Jena said, hoping if she said it enough—and avoided mirrors—she'd believe it.

"You don't look fine. You look like a woman who is

post op bilateral mastectomies. You look like you went and had a major surgery without telling me. Why?"

Jena looked down. "You said you didn't want to know the outcome of my genetic testing. I couldn't very well share my decision to undergo prophylactic bilateral mastectomies without explaining why."

"Prophylactic." Jaci clutched her fist to her heart. "Thank, God." She let out a breath. "I may not have wanted to know the results of your testing, but I most certainly would have wanted to know your plans included surgery. I most certainly would have wanted to be there for you, to listen and research and help you formulate the pros and cons list I'm sure you have stashed somewhere."

In her research folder. Jena smiled.

"When did you have it?"

"Yesterday morning."

"Yesterday morning?" Jaci screeched. "What are you doing home from the hospital? With twins? And Justin? Of all the—"

"I made a terrible mistake." Although she'd thought she was all cried out, new tears flooded Jena's eyes. She dropped her forehead into her palm. "I wanted to be home, but I feel awful, I can't manage my drains by myself and I don't want Justin to see me like this."

"Oh, Jen." Jaci leaned down to give her a gentle hug. It felt so good.

"I think I rushed the surgery." She sucked in a stuttery breath. "Maybe if I'd waited." She looked up at her sister. "Maybe this would be easier if I'd given Justin and me more time together to feel more comfortable around each other." Too late now.

"But Aunt Lynnie." Jaci understood.

"I can see daddy's face when he looked at mom after her surgery. Can't bear to see that look from Justin." Now she ached on the inside, too. "Re...re...repulsed by me."

"Jena Piermont you snap out of it, right now." Jaci knelt on the floor by Jena's feet and put her hand on Jena's knee. "Daddy was an inconsiderate jerk. Justin is a good man."

"I love him," Jena cried.

"I know." Jaci rubbed her back.

"He won't ever love me now." She hated that she sounded so pitiful.

"I think you're mistaken," Jaci said. "He's pretty upset out there. If he's not crazy in love with you already, it's only a matter of time. I'm sure of it. Who wouldn't love you? You're perfect."

Not even close.

Jena reached up to touch her breasts. "I'm half the size I was." She pressed. "And I can't feel anything." But an overwhelming, smothering despair. "They feel dead."

"It's so early in your recovery. Maybe some of the sensation will come back."

And maybe her retained nipples would survive and not fall off. And maybe the scarring would be minimal. And maybe in a few weeks, fully clothed, no one would be able to tell the difference. Maybe. Maybe. Maybe.

"Come on," Jaci said. "Let me take a look at you." And just like that, she shifted into nursing mode, assessing Jena's dressings and drains.

"Thank you, for coming," Jena said, feeling calmer. "I hate to be a bother."

"Stop it," Jaci snapped. "You're my sister. My twin.

I love you." Jaci turned to face her, so serious. "You
have to know how much I love you. You hurt, I hurt.
You're happy, I'm happy. I'd do anything for you, Jena.
Anything."

"You're going to make me cry again," Jena said.

Jaci waved her off. "Then forget I mentioned it."

Not likely.

Jaci washed her hands in the sink.

"Jaci?"

"Yeah."

"I love you, too. And I'd do anything for you, too."

Jaci smiled. "You know, to be quite honest, while
I'm sorry for the circumstances, it feels damn good to
have *you* need me for a change."

Someone knocked on the door. "Everything okay in
there?" Justin asked.

Jena tried to hunch so he wouldn't see her. Something pulled. Ow. "Lock the door."

Jaci did. "Jena's okay. We'll be out in a few minutes."

After Jaci emptied her drains, helped her wash up
and change into a different cotton zip up running suit,
Jena felt much better.

Jena woke up the next morning, after a relatively
good night's sleep—thank you pain medicine—still in
the recliner, where she felt the most comfortable. Justin, who'd refused to sleep in the bed because he didn't
trust her to wake him if she needed him, was asleep on
the couch. Jena got up from the chair, basically feeling
achy all over, and shuffled to the bathroom.

She closed the door, noticed it no longer had a lock,
and opened it. "Really?" she yelled. "That's what you
did after I fell asleep?"

"I figured if you could lock yourself in there then

the girls can," Justin said from the couch. "I'm being a proactive parent."

"Ha ha." She closed the door.

"Do you need me to empty your drains?" Justin asked from the other side of the door.

Too close. "Don't come in."

"I promise to honor your privacy. But if there's an emergency I need to get in there. Now do you need me to empty your drains?"

"No." Jena finished up and washed her hands. "Jaci said she'd stop by before work."

"The nurse said I did a good job of it."

She'd only allowed that because they wouldn't discharge her otherwise, and the minutes she'd spent sitting there while he practiced, trying to make sure he couldn't see under the front of her gown, had been the worst of her entire hospital stay.

"I'd prefer Jaci."

"If that's what you want."

He sounded disappointed. Jena opened the door. "I appreciate you wanting to do it, really. I just feel more comfortable with Jaci."

"A nice big good morning kiss would go a long way toward soothing my hurt feelings." He leaned in and puckered his lips.

Had she really hurt his feelings? No. He had to be teasing. She kissed him.

"Now what would you like for breakfast?"

"You don't have to—"

"I want to," Justin insisted.

So sweet. "How about rye toast and tea?"

"Coming right up."

Over the next few days they fell into a nice routine. Each day Jena felt a bit better and tried to do a bit more, always under Justin's watchful eye. He was absolutely wonderful. But other than an occasional peck of a kiss, she kept her distance, feeling unappealing and unfeminine and not even remotely ready for intimacy of any kind.

One night in the recliner extended into six. And even though Jena's pain decreased and her activity increased, she insisted on sleeping in the recliner chair, claiming it was more comfortable for her than the bed. But with each passing day Justin felt more certain it was her way of putting physical distance between them.

When they sat on the couch to watch television he tried to put his arm around her, she asked him not to. Too sore she'd said. Okay. But he tried to hold her hand and she pulled it away. Tried to flirt and couldn't get one blush out of her.

And those sponge baths the nurse mentioned prior to discharge? The ones he'd gotten kind of excited about? Never happened. Because Jena would only let Jaci in the bathroom with her.

Selfish Justin regretted calling Jaci. But desperately-trying-to-do-the-right-thing fiancé and father Justin accepted that Jena preferred having her sister readily available, whether he liked it or not.

One week after her surgery, Justin drove Jena to the doctor's office to have two of the drains removed, hoping to finally get a look at her chest. Only to spend the duration of the visit, at Jena's request, in the waiting room. Jena had denied him entry into the examination room.

Justin felt her growing more distant, more skittish.

Smiling less. Preoccupied. And he knew in his heart if he didn't do something, he would lose her.

Thinking maybe the first step to getting back the old Jena was to get her out of the condo; he took the opportunity of her doctor's appointment to take her to lunch.

"Why are you stopping here?" she asked as he pulled into a parking lot.

"I'm taking you out to lunch. You've been cooped up in the condo for too long."

"I'm not hungry."

"Well I am."

"I don't want to go." She adjusted her shirt. "I still have two drains. Everyone will see."

He turned to face her. "You are wearing a loose blouse with a bulky sweater. I promise you, the drains and any bandages you may or may not still have are not visible."

He got out of the SUV and walked around to open her door. She looked up at him. Hesitant and unsure. He held out his hand. She placed her hand in his. Thank you. And he helped her out of the car. The first thing she did was tilt her beautiful face up to the sun. "That feels nice."

"Grandma Abbie always used to say the fresh air will do you good."

He tucked her hand in the crook of his arm and led her into the small bistro like any other couple out for a lunch date. It felt good.

The waitress seated them along the wall.

"I feel like everyone is staring at my chest," Jena shared, closing the sides of her sweater.

Justin looked around. "I don't see anyone staring at your chest. Do you?"

Jena looked around. "I guess not."

The waitress took their orders.

"I thought you weren't hungry," Justin teased.

"Well it would be impolite of me to sit here and watch you eat," Jena said primly. Then they lapsed into a casual, comfortable conversation. Jena warmed up and he managed to coax a few smiles and one very distinct blush out of her.

And Justin felt hope.

But back in the condo her don't-touch-me walls shot right back up.

That night after they put the girls to bed Jena said, "I'm going to take a shower."

A shower sounded good to him. "Want some company?"

She reacted like he'd asked her to have kinky sex in front of a room full of men, but quickly regained her composure. "Uh, thank you. But no."

Not one to give up easily he tried a different tack. "Do you need help?"

"No. No." She hurried to the guest bathroom. The guest bathroom. Always the guest bathroom. "I'm good. I'll be fine."

He would have yelled for her to call if she needed anything, but the way things were going, he'd likely hear the thud of her unconscious body hitting the shower floor before she'd call for him. He threw the magazine he'd been reading, frustrated as hell, and he sat there, listening for any signs of distress, imagining rivulets of water flowing down her body, and foam—

Something fell—maybe a shampoo bottle—followed by a groan. He jumped up from the couch, ran to the bathroom, and thank you no more door lock, pushed inside. "Are you okay?"

"A little dizzy." She sounded weak. Dazed.

He threw the shower curtain to the side.

"No!" she screamed. "Go away." She hunched forward and covered her chest. But that meant she had to release her hold on the tub grip bar. She swayed.

Justin reached into the shower spray, turned off the water and scooped her up before she fell.

"Don't look at me," she cried, covering her chest.

Not before he'd seen the purple bruising and the strip of something tape-like over her incisions. And the string from a sweatshirt hood she had tied loosely around her neck with the long tubes of her drains threaded through diaper pins to keep the bulbed ends from dangling.

He sat on the toilet settling Jena on his lap.

"Please, don't look at me," she said again, Quiet. Defeated.

Justin had had enough. "You know what? It's too late. I looked. And you want to know what I saw?"

"No," she said miserably.

"I saw the breasts of a woman I care deeply for looking bruised and painful. And you want to know how it made me feel?"

She shook her head, looking down, almost curled into a ball.

"Tough. You were the one who refused to accept my ring unless I promised to talk to you and be honest with you. So here goes. It makes me feel mad as hell. At cancer. And helpless, that I can't take away the pain or speed your healing. And damn determined." Careful of her drains he draped his arms around hers and hugged her. "I feel you pushing me away and I won't let it happen." Tears pooled in his eyes. She was something special. A keeper. He felt it in his heart. "You can push all you want. But I'm not going anywhere."

Jena said nothing.

"Before your surgery you told me you are more than a pair of breasts. Right on. I agree. What about you? Saying the words isn't enough. You have to believe them." He kissed her head. "You are so much more to me. I love you, Jena. And not solely for your beautiful body, but because of who you are. A smart, sweet, thoughtful, caring, courageous woman."

"I don't feel very courageous at the moment." She lifted her head to look at him. "I love you, too," she admitted. And he'd been right. He'd much rather hear the words come from her mouth than read them on a piece of paper—that now resided in the town dump with the other three letters she'd written. "You've taken such good care of me and the girls."

"I got off to a rocky start."

"But you didn't give up." He wouldn't let himself. "And with everything that went on that night, I think I'd have needed to call in reinforcements, too."

"Thank you." He kissed her forehead.

"You're all wet," Jena said.

"That's what happens when I brave a shower to rescue my fiancée."

"My hero." She smiled. And Justin couldn't help but smile, too.

"You smell like baby shampoo."

"That's what the doctor said to use until I'm all healed."

Which is probably why she always used the guest bathroom. Not because she was avoiding their bedroom, but because they kept the baby shampoo in the guest bathroom where she bathed the twins. And maybe so he'd be close by in case she needed him. "It's starting to harden in your hair."

"I guess I'd better finish my shower."

"About that," he said. "Should I be calling the doctor to tell him you almost passed out?"

She looked away. "He, uh, warned me this might happen."

"And you risked cracking your head open on the tub floor rather than asking me to sit in here with you on the off chance an experienced medical professional may be right?"

"I felt absolutely, totally fine before the shower." She looked up at him with her beautiful blue eyes. "I took care of my mother for years. Trust me. I would not have risked a head injury by taking a shower if I felt the least bit unwell. I honestly thought I'd be fine."

"How do you feel now?" he asked.

"Like I'd appreciate it if you'd sit in here with me while I rinse off."

Good, because no way he was leaving.

"But please," she said, starting to stand. "It makes me uncomfortable for you to look at me right now."

He closed his eyes.

She kissed his cheek. "Thank you."

She turned on the shower. He waited until he heard the curtain close before he opened his eyes. "You okay?"

"Fine."

He lifted his wet shirt over his head, then what the hell, stripped off the rest of his clothes and wrapped a towel around his waist. "Now that you're cleared to take showers, does that mean no more sponge baths?

Cause I was kind of really looking forward to giving you a sponge bath."

She laughed. "You have got to be kidding me. After everything you saw just now, all you're thinking about is giving me a sponge bath?"

As a matter of fact, "Yeah."

"You're amazing," she said.

"Back atcha, baby."

"I like it when you call me baby."

"Why, Jena Piermont. Are you flirting with me?"

She turned off the water. "Please hand me a towel and close your eyes."

Obviously, there was still work to be done. He closed his eyes and opened a large bath towel prepared to wrap her up in it. But they'd made some progress tonight. And progress was good.

Post op week two Jena let him take care of her drains, and she returned to their bed, although she slept out of reach and propped up almost as high as if she was in the recliner. At least he could hold her hand as they drifted off to sleep.

On the next Wednesday they returned to the surgeon's office and Jena's remaining drains were removed. That time he was allowed in the exam room but had to stay on the outside of the curtain. At least he could hear the doctor's evaluation and instructions.

Progress.

Within a few days of drain removal things started to return to normal. Jena could move around better and required less assistance caring for the twins. But by far the best part was she resumed sleeping on her side so he could cuddle up behind her at night. An activity he enjoyed much more than smoking cigars, drinking beer, and playing cards with a bunch of guys into the early morning hours. So when Ryan gave him a hard time for cancelling his fourth poker game in a row, Justin told him to find a permanent replacement to fill his spot. Justin had no interest in playing every week. Here and there maybe, but right now he'd much rather spend his time with his fiancée and daughters.

Toward the end of post op week three it was as if the surgery had never happened. Except he had yet to set eyes on his lovely fiancée's undressed post-surgery body, and they had yet to have sex.

Justin didn't push. But he made it known when she was ready so was he.

Nothing.

So in the middle of post op week four, when he returned home from work, color him totally surprised when Jena greeted him at the door, wearing an instant hardon inducing red babydoll negligee with a matching, sheer, robe, complete with a hint of cleavage, and those silver stilettoes he loved.

"Welcome home," she said with a hesitant smile. Shy. Unsure. She fiddled with her feathered hem. "I thought maybe…" She looked away. "If you wanted…" She swallowed. "We could try…"

"You look fantastic, Jena…amazing." Justin's sex-starved body went hard at the sight of her.

She gifted him with a beautiful smile, walked to him and went up on her toes for a kiss. Not the platonic pecks from the last few weeks. But a real tongue in the mouth, I want you naked now, kind of kiss.

As difficult as it was to do, Justin stopped her.

At her hurt expression he explained, "I have been in some terrible areas today and I need to shower. Five minutes. Tops." He kissed her. Then ran for the shower chanting 'Please don't change your mind. Please don't change your mind. Please don't change your mind.'

He finished in three.

"Now." He hurried into the living room, wearing nothing but a pair of briefs. "Where were we?"

She sat on the corner of the couch with her hands crossed in her lap her feet on the floor, looking prim. And nervous. "The girls are spending the night with Jaci."

Finally. Justin joined her on the couch. Night after night, morning after morning, he'd held her close, aroused and wanting, waiting for her to be ready, waiting for this very moment, waiting to prove how inconsequential breasts had become. Because he loved every enticing, alluring, lovable inch of Jena and was raring to show her.

"Come here." He patted his lap.

She looked over at him. "I'm not sure how this will turn out. But we need to get past this first awkward time if there's any hope…" She turned her head. "I want to make you happy, to give you what you need. But…"

"You do make me happy," he said. "Please." He reached for her arm. "What I need right now is to hold you close." To calm her nerves, rouse her passion and build her confidence.

In a show of trust that humbled him, she climbed over to straddle his lap. "Is this okay?"

He was so desperate to have her, hanging by their feet from the ceiling would have been okay. He nodded, placed his hands on her hips and guided her down.

Her eyes went wide with surprise when she settled on top of his erection.

"You feel what you do to me?" he asked, rocking beneath her, feeling her body relax. Good. "I want you just as much now as I did before."

"Kiss me," she said seconds before she set her lips to his.

Soft. Warm. Moist. Tentative. Justin channeled every bit of his love, relief, and hope for the future into the kiss he gave her back, careful not to squeeze her as tight as he wanted for fear he'd hurt her.

When Jena broke away, breathing heavy, looking slightly dazed, she said, "I love the way you kiss me." She touched a finger to her lips. "I didn't think it'd be enough but…" She rocked her hips. Tears formed in her eyes. "That feels so good."

Justin massaged her through her panties, slid his hands up under her satin and lace teddy, down to her butt, pressed her down, swiveled, teetered on the verge of bursting.

She rubbed along his length. He stayed her hips. "Baby you don't want to do that right now. Lift up."

Jena did and he shimmied out of his boxers.

When she sat back down he met her bare sex. What the…? He looked down. When had she removed those sexy red panties?

"They have an opening. For you to…" She blushed.

Justin hoped she'd never stopped blushing for him. He thrust up. Made contact. So damn good.

"I'm on birth control," she said. "And since both our STD panels came out negative…" She sank down, taking him inside of her, naked skin to glorious hot, wet, naked skin. His first time ever and it felt so good Justin wasn't sure he'd survive it.

She leaned forward to whisper in his ear. "I'm not

sure if I mentioned how much I appreciate all your understanding and patience over the past few weeks."

She had.

"Or how lucky I am to have you as my soon-to-be husband."

Yup. But he didn't mind hearing it again.

"Or how much I love you."

Now that he'd never get tired of hearing. "I love you, too, Jena."

In a move that far exceeded her experience she jerked her hips and took him even deeper, making using his big brain near impossible. He fought to remain focused on the conversation.

Unsuccessfully.

He gripped her butt, withdrew and surged back in then pulled her down for a kiss. "Thank you for choosing me as your one and only." He started to lift her teddy, needing to see all of her, to show her he was okay with the changes to her body, that they didn't matter. Because he loved her.

"No," she said, holding it in place. "I'd prefer to leave it on."

Perfectly fine, as long as she didn't push him away. "Did I mention my fondness for sexy negligees?" He caressed the smooth, luxurious wisp of fabric covering her belly.

"I've got dozens of them."

And Justin couldn't wait to see and feel and snuggle up against every single one of them.

EPILOGUE

Two weeks later

"You look beautiful," Jaci said to Jena.

"So do you," Jena replied. Identical, in fact, from their matching ivory wedding gowns in simple, under-stated, tasteful, elegance to their updos, makeup and manicures.

"Mom would love that we're getting married here."

In her beautiful garden. "Thank you for suggesting it." Insisting actually, just as she'd insisted on wait-ing to get married until Jena was all healed and ready to participate in a double ceremony. "I feel like she's here with us."

Jaci looked around and smiled. "Me, too."

Jena would forever be indebted to her stubborn sis-ter who'd refused to let her be content with a quickie courthouse wedding.

"Is that harp music I hear?"

Jaci listened. Then smiled. "Surprise!" She bounced on the tippy-toes of her pricy pumps. "I couldn't help myself. I'd seen her at Patsy's wedding last year. I came across her card while looking for a ring I'd misplaced. I called her and she had room in her schedule. It was meant to be."

"You did it," Jena said. While she'd been preoccupied by the twins, Justin and adjusting to her new body and her new life to realize. "Except for the hundreds of guests and mom being here, you've put together my dream wedding." Right down to the harpist. "How did you know?"

Jaci picked at her bouquet. "You only talked about it incessantly when we were teenagers."

"I didn't think you listened."

"Well I did," Jaci said. "Over the years your fantasy kind of became my fantasy, too." She shrugged. "So here we are."

"I love you." Jena hugged her sister. "And I don't care if you wrinkle."

"I love you back." Jaci squeezed her tight. "I want you to be happy."

Jena stepped out of their embrace. "I am." So happy. So in love. So blessed. "And I want you to be happy, too."

"I am." Jaci smiled.

"Well," Jena said. "Neither one of us thought it possible, but we both managed to find great guys who love us as much as we love them. Despite daddy's mandate."

"And Jerry's underhanded maneuvering."

No. Their childhoods weren't perfect. But with each new generation came the opportunity for change. "I won't ever force my girls into marriage. Or allow either one of them to give up their childhood to take on adult responsibilities just to make my life easier."

Jaci set her hand on her flat belly and looked down at it. "And I won't allow my children to ever feel the pain and degradation of physical abuse. I will accept them and love them, faults and all, no matter how wild or badly they behave or how much they act out."

"How could I not have seen it?" Jena said, eying Jaci's protective, loving caress of her abdomen. "You're pregnant!"

Jaci smiled and nodded.

"Oh, Jaci." Jena wrapped her arms around her sister again. "I'm so happy for you. Now our children will be close in age. They'll grow up together and be best friends."

"Which is exactly what I wanted. But please, don't say anything. I'm going to tell Ian tonight."

"Dah-lings, you look mah-velous." Aunt Mill, who'd spared no expense dressing up for the wedding and looked very Hollywood glamorous, walked down the stone pathway to where they stood. Out of hiding from her abusive husband just for the day, Jena and Jaci had decided having Aunt Mill at their ceremony was more important than any other local guests. "It's time to go." She reached them, turned around, and held out an elbow to each of them. "Your young men are getting antsy. I need Jena on the right and Jaci on the left."

Jena looked at Jaci. And Jaci looked and Jena. And with sweet smiles they switched places.

Completely unaware, Aunt Mill led them down the pathway.

"I can feel your mother all around us." Aunt Mill looked up to the clear blue sky and inhaled deeply. "As she was before the cancer and the head injury and she is exuberant."

A fragrant breeze blew past.

They turned a corner and Ian, Justin, and the judge who would be performing the ceremony, came into view.

Marta stood to the right beside Justin, holding Abbie

and Annie. Mandy stood to the left beside Ian, holding Maddie.

Justin, so handsome in his tuxedo, looked back and forth between her and Jaci.

Ian, looking equally handsome, winked at Jena then focused in on his real bride.

Aunt Mill stopped about five feet from the men.

Justin looked at Ian who motioned for him to go first so he walked toward Jaci and Jena's heart squeezed. After all they'd been through together he still couldn't recognize her. He extended his hand palm up in front of Jaci. Jena debated what to do. But at the last possible second, he turned toward Jena and quietly said, "I believe I'm supposed to be marrying you today, Jena, unless you've changed your mind."

Joy fluttered just under her skin. "I haven't." She took his hand and accompanied him to stand before the judge.

A warm, fragrant breeze enveloped her in love and Jena knew, without a doubt, her mom was in attendance.

Abbie started to fuss.

Justin made a move toward Marta then stopped himself.

The judge started to speak.

Abbie started to cry.

"She's not going to stop until you hold her," Jena whispered.

And sure enough Justin took Abbie into his arms and she immediately went quiet.

"Sorry," Justin said.

The judge continued.

Then Annie started to cry.

Jena took her from Marta and she immediately went quiet.

"Sorry," Jena said.

The judge continued.

After they repeated their vows and as the judge said, "You may now kiss your brides," Justin handed Abbie back to Marta and took Annie and handed her to Marta, and over their cries of protest said to Jena, "I love our girls, but some moments aren't meant to be shared." And he took her in his arms and kissed her.

During the small luncheon at Jaci's condo—because Aunt Mill couldn't be seen out in public—that followed, Jena whispered in her husband's ear, "I forgot to tell you, your package arrived this morning while you were at the store." The surprise present he'd ordered for her to wear on their wedding night.

Since Jena preferred to keep her foobs—fake boobs—under wraps, she and Justin had taken up the fun and surprisingly stimulating hobby of searching out enticing negligees and arousing outfits for her to wear to bed.

Justin smiled that smile that never failed to put her in the mood. "I can't wait to see you in it," he whispered back with a quick swipe of his tongue in her ear.

"And I can't wait to see you see me in it." Modeling for Justin turned out to be a highly erotic form of foreplay they both enjoyed, and Jena loved to watch his lust-filled eyes when she performed for him.

Their sex life had changed, but was no less satisfying than it'd been before surgery. Jena couldn't remember what aroused nipples felt like, and she didn't miss them at all.

* * * * *

& A sneaky peek at next month...

Medical Romance

CAPTIVATING MEDICAL DRAMA—WITH HEART

My wish list for next month's titles...

In stores from 1st February 2013:

☐ The Brooding Doc's Redemption — Kate Hardy

& An Inescapable Temptation — Scarlet Wilson

☐ Revealing The Real Dr Robinson — Dianne Drake

& The Rebel and Miss Jones — Annie Claydon

☐ The Son that Changed his Life — Jennifer Taylor

& Swallowbrook's Wedding of the Year — Abigail Gordon

Available at WHSmith, Tesco, Asda, Eason, Amazon and Apple

Just can't wait?